Honey Sweetheart

By

Lacy Enderson

ISBN-13: 978-0-9777417-3-1

CONTENTS

FORWARD

Where exactly *is* the Christian teen's place in this sometimes scary thing called 'adulthood' while dealing with the powerful pull of the world?

The protagonist of this latest book by Lacy Enderson, *Honey Sweetheart,* breaths new life into what is for young people, a time of exploration and difficult decisions.

Most parents can readily identify their own teenagers in this book, as they attempt to navigate through the thorns and thistles while society proclaims that "These are the happiest years of your life." *Are they really?*

While battling the onslaughts of low self esteem, *Honey Sweetheart* becomes a cheerleader who is astonished to find herself not only becoming popular but igniting some jealousy- based resentment toward her from other girls.

No matter what she did she felt like a pathetic loser. That is, until she was invited to a party, with other party invitations quickly lining up.

After twenty parties, this formerly quiet shy introvert transformed into an outgoing fun loving member of the "in-crowd." She was in such a whirl-wind that she lost her balance between her family, home life, and her church as her new life, seemingly demanded of her peers, crowded out all the other areas.

A teen-aged son or daughter struggling against the currents of the world can be suddenly swept out to a sea of immorality, declining honesty and compromising ideals, losing their compass while their parents are left bewildered. It is a pleasant read to see how all of this turns out. *Both parents and teens will benefit from this work.*

Lacy Enderson is one of the few authors who do more than writing the story. She takes the reader inside the head of the subjects she writes about so one can fully grasp the forces at work in these lives, all based on actual people.

Her earlier book, *"Addiction: A Personal Story"* chronicles her own life of dependency, taking the readers into her own head as she schemed, planned and manipulated before eventually being set free. She wrote with such transparency that some might have hesitated to read further since her story was so personal and open.

This reviewer found her book the best for counselors and chaplains ever written, precisely because of the understanding she gives of the mind of an addict. Many copies of her book are given to chaplains in training and ministers being mentored as well as Pastors.

Ms. Enderson also published a book titled: "So You Want To Lose Weight but You Can't Stop Eating" She has earned her Master of Arts Degree in Biblical Counseling, is currently completing a Masters of Divinity Degree and is devoting her time to helping others through the snares of life.

Rev. Austin Miles
Chaplain-Author, Writer and reviewer of books, TV shows and concerts.

HELLO IT'S ME

Hello, my name is Honey Sweetheart. I guess that means I'm supposed to be sweet. Although most of the time I'm not.

"Why, mom, did you name her that?" my sisters often asked. "She's not sweet. She's mean. She picks on us endlessly and we don't like it."

It doesn't bother me when they say things like that, most of the time they're right. It's hard to be a teenager in this world. I get frustrated a lot and sometimes I'm anything but sweet. I'll work on it though, even if just to live up to my namesake.

I'm seventeen, a senior in high school, and although I'm told this should be the happiest year of my life, I can't exactly say I feel very happy. Most days I'm just content if I'm not depressed. I hear it's normal for a teenage girl to feel depressed. I hope I outgrow it.

I live in a small town outside Los Angeles. I go to a private high school nearby my home. My mom home-schooled me during elementary school, and I attended a small Christian Charter school during middle school. I did try a public high school for one day, but a private school is definitely where I belong.

My parents raised me in a Christian home. Sunday school on Sunday mornings was mandatory. Wednesday nights I attended youth group, and Friday nights it was GMG (Girls Meeting God).

I lived a secluded life. My friends were either from my church or the kids from my school who went to other churches. Prior to middle school, all of my education took place at home. The only interaction I had with kids my age was at church, church events, and church camps.

Before the first day of my freshman year my mom struggled daily trying to decide what school to send me to. She feared I wouldn't fit in with the kids at the public school. She told me they were different.

"Oh mom, how much different could they be?"

But she was right. They were different, very different.

The first day of public high school I was sitting in my homeroom class when some boy yelled across the room, "Hey you? Who are you? I've never seen you before. What're you doing here? Are you weird? You look weird."

Then he called me a word I'd never heard before. It was probably an obscene word by the way all the kids started laughing, and how the teacher sternly escorted him from the room. I was mortified and began to cry.

After homeroom I hid in a bathroom stall and called my mom, "Hurry mom. Come rescue me from this horrible place."

I wasn't used to boys calling me names. In fact, up until then, only my sisters ever called me names. A boy calling me names was dreadful. I wanted to die.

"Mom," I begged. "Please home-school me." The more I begged the more adamant she was.

"You're too old to be home-schooled, and it's time you made new friends."

She so badly wanted me to get along with other kids; to quit being afraid; to start living instead of hiding all the time. I tried. I wanted to be like other kids.

After tremendous amounts of begging, my mom finally enrolled me in a private Christian school. "That's the best I can do," she said.

"Thanks mom. Thank you so much." I was both grateful and relieved.

The first day of my new school was already a week into the semester. The students had already chosen the best seats and gathered into their so-called cliques. I sat in the back during my first class oblivious to what was going on. All I wanted to do was to go home and hide under my bed. I hated school--all schools, and I never wanted to face this horrible place again.

I called my mom from the corner of an empty cafeteria, but this time mom wasn't coming to my rescue. She wasn't coming to save me and there was no changing her mind.

"Please mom, teach me at home!" I cried.

"I am not home-schooling you. I want you in school, and that is the last word on the subject. You are going to school."

Accepting high school didn't happen overnight. It took a few weeks to get used to things. Eventually I found a small group of girls I felt comfortable with, and before long, I settled in.

It's been almost four years since I first started high school. Of course school has its ups and downs, but I learned to accept that a day was coming when I would graduate and move on. That's my goal and it's actually only a few months away. It's hard to believe, but school is almost over.

It's been a rough road for me as a Christian in high school. The rules changed and kids were different; less obedient. Temptation was never really a problem back then. I was just never tempted. I mean nothing out of the ordinary. There were a few movies I wasn't allowed to see, but other than that, not much.

It's normal for kids to rebel. I think we're born that way. I fought with my mom over everything: make-up; how low the waistband on my jeans was; not letting my sisters in my room; making sure the dog got outside before he wet all over the floor. We fought over whether I could drive my friends in my car when I first got my license. I knew the rules, but I fought with her anyway.

I remember once wanting to go to the beach with friends on a day when I had softball practice. I knew my dad would forbid it, but I asked my mom anyway, and when she said no, I got mad. I didn't speak to her for two weeks--now, how mean is that?

I was bad at commitments. I was always joining some new team, but the same thing happened every time--I felt out of place and I quit. I was the first one in line at the start of every season, and I always heard my mom's voice like a whisper in my ear, "Are you sure? Now Honey, make sure you are absolutely certain before you join that team."

Do teenagers have brain damage? Do we have faulty memories? For the life of me I kept making this same mistake over and over again.

Anything I ever wanted was handed to me on a silver platter, but once it was mine, I didn't want it anymore. My friends envied me. "You are spoiled rotten," they'd say. "You are the most unappreciative person we know." And they were right. I was used to getting what I wanted.

Taking my parents for granted became a habit--a very bad habit.

FALLING DOWN GRACEFULLY

I first noticed Trevor near the end of my junior year. I paid very little attention to boys up until then, but this year was different. I decided to try out for cheerleading, and they held the tryouts near the field where the track team ran. Trevor didn't run on the track team, but he came out to watch his friends. Or maybe he hung out to watch the girls. Whatever the reason, I looked forward to seeing him.

I wasn't very popular. I chose not to be. I spent most of my time making sure no one knew me, and other than a few friends, no one did. I was good at playing invisible. I walked with my head down, and looked up only when I needed to.

I did have a few girlfriends I adored; you know the ones that finish your sentences. We did everything together. But they weren't trying out for cheerleading. Their parents said no.

I hesitated at first, because I didn't know the girls trying out, but I really wanted to be a cheerleader. Of course my mom worried that I'd made another commitment I wouldn't follow through with, but I committed anyway.

I made a promise to myself to stay with the team no matter what. I wanted to prove my mom wrong. I went to cheer tryouts everyday and did the best I could, even though most of the girls were much better than me.

My favorite part of practice was watching the boys and knowing they were watching us. Although I knew they weren't watching me, I was excited to be with a group of girls who got so much attention. No one ever paid me any attention—I never wanted any—but indirectly the attention was nice.

Trevor seemed a little quieter than the other guys--maybe that is why I noticed him. Whatever the reason, I noticed him more and more. I saw him at lunch, and walking through the halls, so I followed him—all the time. Before long I was looking for him everywhere. He quickly became my new obsession.

I didn't know anything about Trevor. He looked and acted decent. He attended a Christian school. I thought that was a good sign. I wasn't too concerned since I wasn't planning on marrying him. In fact, I chose to keep my feelings a secret. I quietly kept my distance, and enjoyed him from afar.

I thought boys were cute, but I wasn't boy crazy. I survived without a boyfriend for a long time. I was certain to be just fine without one now. None of my friends had boyfriends either--we didn't have time for them. We were too busy hanging out at the mall, or lying out by my pool.

After I made the cheerleading team I discovered Trevor played football--what a coincidence. I was cheering for him.

I had a great summer. I spent a lot of time with my new friends--they were a lot of fun. I didn't spend as much time with my old friends, and that caused some problems.

There were these two girls on the cheer team who were really stuck up and they didn't like outsiders hanging around. That caused a huge problem for me. Brenda and Charlene came from a wealthy part of town near the school. They weren't very tolerant of average girls like my best friends.

I admit my friends weren't the best looking girls in school, but that was never a problem for me. I didn't pick my friends based on beauty. I chose them because they were fun and they honestly cared about me.

Brenda and Charlene both drove BMW's and had the most recent and high-tech cell phones. I often wondered what their parents were thinking.

Most of the girls on the team came from well-off families, but all the other girls had kind and humble hearts. They weren't proud and arrogant. Brenda and Charlene were different. They made it very clear that anyone not on the team wasn't welcome in their group.

My parents raised me conservatively. We had just as much money as the other families from my school, but I was taught that it wasn't the material items that mattered; it was about what was in the heart. My parents taught me to love and accept all people regardless of their financial position. It was obvious Brenda and Charlene weren't taught the same values.

During the summer, Courtney, a girl on the cheer team, decided to have a swimming party. Only the girls on the team were invited, but I wanted Amelia and Cindy there. We didn't spend much time together anymore and I knew their feelings were hurt. I hoped inviting them to the party would help mend our friendship. The friction between us bothered me and I hated that we were growing apart.

Being a cheerleader was a whole new way of life for me. I enjoyed cheering more than anything else--this was my niche. It was just unfortunate that my new world was so far away from my two best friends.

The day of the party was a catastrophe. I remember it like it was yesterday. Amelia and Cindy, although hesitant at first, gladly accepted the invitation to the party. The closer the party day came, the more excited they grew.

My friends and I suffered from the same low self esteem--I think it was an epidemic--so the thought of spending the day with the most popular girls in school did not sit well with them at first. But after a while they were more excited than I saw them in a long time.

A few hours before the party Brenda found out I invited my friends. She wasn't happy. In fact, she was so unhappy, she made Courtney un-invite them. She told Amelia and Cindy that too many people were coming already. Courtney said there wasn't enough room for them.

"How could she do that?" I asked my mom. "How could anyone be so cruel?"

I could hardly look at them. They were so upset. I felt like such a pathetic loser. I contemplated staying home myself, but reality sunk in. This was my new group of friends. This was who I'd spend my entire senior year with.

That summer I attended at least twenty parties. I transformed from a quiet, shy, introvert, into an outgoing, fun loving member of the in-crowd.

It was hard to believe that the most popular girls in school accepted me. I mean, these were the girls every other girl in school wanted to be. But they not only accepted me as a team member, they were my friends. They called and invited me everywhere they went.

I tried to find a balance between my home life, church life, school life, and my new life, but somehow my new life crowded out every other area of my life. I remember my sister Hope sending me a message on my computer. It simply read, "I miss you!" I cried.

I felt bad about neglecting my family, but I was becoming a new person. Isn't that what my mom wanted? For years she told me, "You're too shy. You need to come out of your shell. You need to develop more confidence, participate in new activities, and meet new people." So that's what I did.

I finally listened to my mom, yet she wasn't very happy with me. No one in my family seemed happy with me anymore. A battle raged between my head and my heart, and my heart was losing.

My mom called me stuck up. She said she didn't even know me anymore. She told me she was unhappy with the way I treated my family, and wanted me to spend more time at home.

"But why," I shouted. "No one is ever doing anything together. Dad is always in his den working, and you are usually in your room sewing. My sisters don't want me hanging around—they're my sisters. They're not supposed to."

My mom warned me daily to quit picking on them. "I'll lock you in your room and isolate you from your new friends," she said. "They are bad influences, and I'm not so sure cheerleading was such a good idea."

"But what else am I going to do?" I argued.

"You're a beautiful girl, but you let this popularity thing go to your head. It's time to get off your high horse and come down to reality. I just don't know what's gotten into you. You were such a sweet girl," she continued. "Now all you do is pester your sisters. You haven't said one nice word to either one of them since you made the cheer team. I think it was a big mistake, and if I hadn't spent so much money on camp and uniforms, I would pull you out right now. I'm definitely disappointed in you."

My mom used the word disappointed. I hated that word.

I was not a disappointment. I got straight A's on my report card every year. I went to church with her every Sunday and youth group every Wednesday night—well, maybe not as often as I used to, but I still went often enough.

I told her it was unfair to judge me so harshly. "You were a cheerleader too. You changed too when you were a cheerleader--everyone changes."

But I knew better. Not only did my mom cheer, she was also the football homecoming queen--my dream. But she was right. My mom was a remarkable woman. She had a huge heart for other people and I sensed nothing ever went to her head. I knew my mom never changed.

Trevor was at quite a few of the early summer parties. Most of them were for the cheer and football teams combined. I saw Trevor a lot, but I never let on that I liked him. Not at first anyway. I enjoyed him from a distance, the way I preferred. I carried his picture around with me everywhere I went, "Isn't he cute Aunt Stacey? Isn't he cute grandma?"

I still didn't know much about him. I heard through some kids at school he liked to play cards and drink beer. I didn't like hearing that. I never drank beer and I certainly didn't hang around with friends who did. But was there really any harm in drinking beer?

I was told by his closest friend he only drank occasionally, so I brushed it off as no big deal. Wasn't I taught 'judge not lest I be judged?' And I wasn't perfect either. Occasionally I picked on my sisters, and disobeyed my parents. Wasn't that a sin?

Over the next few months I heard quite a few disturbing details about Trevor's behavior, but each and every bit of information I shrugged off as unimportant. I had more fun fantasying about the way I wanted Trevor to be, rather than accepting the facts of who he really was. It didn't matter anyway. I wasn't planning on dating him.

My life was far too busy for a boyfriend, and I didn't understand why anyone wanted the aggravation of having one around. I knew I didn't.

DELICATELY DISAPPOINTING

One week each summer my family rented a beach house. The house was always the same one--on a quiet beach near Malibu. It was rather large, with four bedrooms and two beds in each room--plenty of space for a lot of people.

My sisters and I were allowed to invite one friend each. My mom said I could invite two friends if I promised to invite Amelia and Cindy and no one from the cheer team. I said that was fair. I needed to spend more time with my two best friends anyway, and this week was a great time to bond again.

Each year I looked forward to lying out on the beach, in the sun, all day long. Of course my mom harped at me constantly about how bad the sun was for my skin, but I didn't care. It was my favorite part of summer vacation: lying in the sun, lost in my thoughts, getting a dark tan. The weather at the beach was beautiful--the sky was clear, and the sun was hot. I knew it was going to be a perfect week.

I also knew right away this year would be different. This year there were boys. I know there were always boys. I just never noticed them before. Amelia and Cindy were just as excited as I was. I guess we were finally growing up. And it didn't take long for the boys to notice us too. Within a few very short hours three of them were sitting on our blanket asking questions and carrying on small talk.

I was not sure who was more attractive to them--me or my friends. I was told I was far better looking than both of them. I just never developed enough confidence to believe that. But that didn't stop me. I had my eye on the cutest boy of the bunch, and I was determined to get his attention.

His name was Curt. He was quite a bit older than the other boys, with shoulder length brown hair and beautiful blue eyes. He wore his hair parted on the side and it curled a little bit on the ends. His friends wore their hair long too, but they had bleached blonde hair from the sun. They looked more like your typical California surfer.

Don't misunderstand; there was nothing wrong with the way they looked. They just didn't have the same sophisticated, charming, and handsome looks as Curt did. And I don't think they were as old either, because they acted very immature. I spent most of my time gazing at Curt out of the corner of my eye, so as not to seem too obvious.

One afternoon as we sat on the beach talking and laughing—or should I say giggling—I could see my mom in the distance approaching fast.

"Hi girls," she said. "Who do we have here?" She was obviously concerned. Curt was definitely too old for me.

I gave my mom one of those go away glares, so she reluctantly went back to the beach house. But I was certain there was a lecture waiting for me when I returned.

Amelia and Cindy were quite content spending time with Curt's friends—Jarrod and Taylor—and I didn't want my mom ruining that for them. The boys were all very nice. There was no need for her to worry.

Back at the beach house my lecture was waiting. My mom tried to tell me that boys Curt's age were up to no good. She proceeded to tell me all about the boy in school who took advantage of her when she least expected it. She said there was never a boy that age with any good intentions, and I was much better off keeping my distance.

"Act aloof," she said, "and eventually the boys will go away."

I know my mom was older and wiser. I even admitted she was probably right, but seriously, what was wrong with her? I had met a really cute boy. She was supposed to be happy for me.

"Mom, you have no idea who Curt is or what his intentions are. You have no business judging him because of other boys his age." I was clearly disturbed and certainly let her know. "I can't believe you would ruin this for me."

As I stormed off to my room I called out to my friends, "Come on Amelia and Cindy."

We spent the rest of the evening up in the room planning our next devious move. Maybe she thought she won, but we knew better. I refused to let her interfere in our week. This was our vacation too.

My friends and I spent the remaining days lying out in the sun watching the boys surf. Occasionally they joined us on the beach for conversation. On Thursday morning we got up extra early while it was still overcast and cold. The boys started surfing early and we wanted to be there when they showed up. We wore our bathing suits to attract attention, but we had to wrap up tight in our towels—it was cold that morning on the beach.

Unfortunately they came late. It seemed like forever. The butterflies raced around in my stomach every time I thought about Curt, and the waiting was driving me crazy—it was an unfamiliar yet wonderful feeling.

I felt that way a little bit around Trevor, but not the same. Curt was exciting. He was older and very good-looking. Trevor was closer to my age, and clearly more appropriate for me. Trevor was good-looking too, but not nearly as handsome. Curt was much older, more mature, and definitely off limits. I was so confused.

It was obvious we were waiting for them, and I was a little embarrassed. But I really didn't care. I knew the time to spend with Curt was limited, and I didn't want to waste one second hindered by ridiculous school-girl feelings.

As soon as Curt saw us he waved and came over. His friends went on ahead into the water, but Curt came over and sat down. He didn't necessarily sit next to me, he just sat down.

I sensed he was trying not to play favorites. It seemed like a nice thing to do, but it was all so confusing. Did he like me? Did he like one of my friends? I just wanted to know. *Hey Curt*, I thought to myself, *Do you like me*?

After a few minutes of small talk he invited us back to his place. He asked if we wanted to see where he lived. We said yes. Why not? I was curious to know where he lived. Maybe someday I would want to see him again? How could I visit if I didn't know where he lived? The promise I made to my mom was to stay on the beach, but as soon as he invited us to his house, I forgot all my promises.

The beach area was small, so his house was quite close to the one we were renting--all the houses were within walking distance to the beach, and to each other. His home was a typical beat up old beach house. I heard that the sea air was bad for the paint which is why most of the houses looked old and drab. His was no exception.

The house was an obvious bachelor pad. There were no decorations, or pictures on the walls. The walls were white, and laundry was scattered all over the floor. Thrown in the corners of the living room were overstuffed pillows and bean bag chairs. A television sitting on a milk crate was the only other piece of furniture in the room. His home was definitely in need of a woman's touch.

I wondered where his mom was. I thought all moms decorated their children's homes--especially a son's. It seemed boys were always in need of their mother's help, but then so was I.

Matching the color of my carpet to the paint on my walls was impossible for me, yet my mom knew exactly what wall hangings went with the wallpaper and where exactly to hang each picture. I did not inherit her talent.

My thoughts raced on, non stop, and I quietly thanked God that Curt was not a mind reader. Because if he was, he would know I was nothing more than a scared, immature teenager. I mean, seriously, what was so important about his mom right now and the color of his walls?

Suddenly I felt very uncomfortable, but even more-so, I feared my mom would discover we left the beach and send for the police. Certainly she would worry if we were gone.

And what if my sisters showed up at the beach early and discovered we weren't there? Surely they'd run back and tell my mom. "Honey and her friends are not at the beach." I knew I was in serious trouble.

My stomach wasn't well. I started feeling sick. My heart was racing and I couldn't think straight. I needed to leave. I didn't want to leave--I wanted to stay. I wanted to stay in that house with Curt forever. I never wanted to leave. But I knew I had to.

I didn't know what was happening. I felt strange. *Was this love?* This was not love--how silly. I had only known Curt for a few days. I did not love him. It was definitely nothing more than a school-girl crush.

I wanted this feeling to last forever, yet at the same time, I needed it to go away. It was making me sick. I wanted to stay, but I knew I had to get out of there.

My friends showed no interest in Curt. They had no problem going in and sitting down. I knew the feeling. The guys I didn't like were the easiest to talk to. I carried on the best conversations with the guys I had no feelings for. But this was not the case today. I was a nervous wreck. I was extremely weak and uncomfortable and I finally told Curt it was time to go.

Amelia and Cindy had no idea what was wrong with me, but stood up anyway and went to the door. I think they saw it in my face that something was terribly wrong.

Cindy and Amelia went ahead of me, and I was almost there when Curt called out "Honey." When I turned around he grabbed my arm and kissed me. I just stood there confused. I had no idea he even liked me. He hid his feelings well.

Curt kissed me for what felt like an eternity, and when he let me go, I didn't want him to.

He just stood there staring at me. "Honey," he said, "please stay."

I tried to explain if my mom caught me in his house I'd be grounded for the rest of my life. We only had two more days to spend at the beach and I didn't want to ruin it. Reluctantly, I turned around, and we left.

I ran at least three feet ahead of my friends without saying a word. I really had no words for what just happened. Instead of going back to the beach, we went back to the house. I needed to make sure everything was okay with my mom, and it was.

I knew my friends wanted an explanation, but I needed some time to sit and think. I needed to be alone. I hated being young. Curt probably thought of me as a juvenile adolescent and I wished I was older. I wished I was nineteen.

I was emotionally numb. My whole body ached. I curled up in a fetal position on the couch and cried. My heart hurt. My head hurt, and I felt empty inside.

Amelia and Cindy were confused. "Honey, what's wrong? Don't you like him? We thought you liked him? We thought you wanted to be with him? Why are you so sad?"

"I wish Jerrod would kiss me," Amelia shouted.

"You don't understand," I told them. "I finally met a great guy, and he even likes me back, but I'm going home in two days and I will never see him again."

I didn't care that Curt was older than me, and I didn't care what my mom said. All I cared about was meeting the boy of my dreams and knowing I was leaving him forever. No kiss in the world was going to change that fact.

I curled up on the couch for two hours until I finally fell asleep. The way I felt, sleep was my only option. When I woke up I still felt lost and alone. I wanted to feel the excitement of a first kiss with a great guy, but I wasn't excited. I was empty.

I thought about Trevor back at home, and how much I liked him. *I think I'll just keep him at a distance forever. No sense setting myself up for more heartache.*

The next day was a little easier, not a lot, just a little. I woke up early fully aware it was our last day of vacation. I decided to go the beach, lie out in the sun, and daydream about magical places I wanted to visit someday. I tried to think about Rome, but I could not stop thinking about Curt. I tried to think of exotic places, but thoughts of Curt prevailed.

The beach was fairly empty that day--just my two friends and I and a few scattered people reading books and taking naps. It was definitely one of the more quiet days. Off in the distance I saw people coming towards us. The sun was in my eyes so at first I couldn't see them, but as they neared, I saw it was Curt and his friends.

Oh my Gosh, I thought. *What should I do?*

I laid there very still. A pit welled up in my stomach and I thought I was going to be sick. Before I had time to react, Curt was lying on my towel with his face two inches from mine.

"Honey Sweetheart, why did you leave? I wanted you to stay. I can't believe you're leaving tomorrow. I wanted to spend the whole night with you."

What was he talking about? What was he thinking? I could never spend all night with him even if I wanted to. My mom would lock me in my room for the rest of my life. Couldn't he see how difficult this was for me? Didn't he know I was only sixteen? Why did he want me anyway? I tried to get up but he held me down, staring intently into my eyes.

I thought to myself, *If only he were ugly. If only he had ugly orange hair and crooked teeth. If only he were unattractive I would tell him to go away.*"

But he wasn't ugly, he was gorgeous, and I was smitten. I gave in. "Come join me," I said.

"Absolutely," he replied.

We sat on the beach and talked for hours; we talked about everything. I told him I made the cheerleading team, and I think he was impressed. A few times he asked me to go back to his house, but of course I said no. As much as I wanted to go with him I just knew that was the wrong thing to do.

Maybe I was a young, naïve sixteen year old, but I wasn't stupid. Going back to his place meant only one thing, and that definitely wasn't going to happen. My mom was right, and I knew it. Nothing good ever came out of being alone in a house with a nineteen year old boy. Saying no was hard, but I'm glad I did.

Of course, looking back now, I see how silly the whole thing was. A long time ago I made a pact with God to remain pure until marriage. I know it seems primitive, but it's important to me.

It's funny how easily I forgot God when faced with a decision concerning my flesh. I heard a pastor preach once on the issue of the 'flesh crying out'. Now I knew what he meant. My flesh was crying out very loudly.

Nineteen year old boys have only one thing on their minds, unless of course they love Jesus and put God first. I never knew a guy, except those who vowed purity, who didn't want to have sex with every girl he met. Curt was no exception. I feared my heart would never mend, but it did.

My family left the beach the next day, and although it was hard at the time, I survived. I am not going to lie, it took a few weeks, but eventually I settled back into my own little world of cheerleading and Trevor.

I made an effort to spend more time with Amelia and Cindy. I also tried to spend more time at home with my mom and my sisters. Most importantly I went to youth group every Wednesday night, not just occasionally.

One thing was certain, as I got older, my need for God definitely increased. I realized as a teenage girl in high school, I was going to need God's help more now than ever before.

ALL IN A DAZED CONFUSION

Courtney told me Trevor asked about me while I was gone. Honestly, I was shocked. I had no idea he even knew I existed. Maybe it was time to make my move. If Trevor already liked me, then what did I have to lose?

I wanted to feel good about the news, but I felt worse. I kept thinking, *Here we go again...and so soon.* Because I knew he liked me, I began avoiding him everywhere I went. It used to be easy, now it was hard. I just wanted to protect my heart. Was that so wrong?

On the fourth of July, of that year, Matt--one of the boys from the football team-- had a huge summer backyard barbeque. I think the whole school was there. I mean, seriously, there were so many people at his house I didn't know who wasn't there.

Of course Amelia and Cindy were there too. I made sure of that. Brenda and Charlene had no right to say who was invited to someone else's party—football team or not. Brenda dated Matt for a short time the year prior, but not anymore. The party was announced as 'anyone is invited,' and I must say, I think everyone was there.

Matt had a huge pool in his backyard with a diving board and a slide. Kids played volleyball in the pool, and in the yard. Others floated on blow-up rafts and inner tubes. It was funny to see croquet set out on the lawn. I thought only grown-ups played croquet.

Quite a few of the guys gathered in the living room to play video games. "What's up with the video games?" I asked Amelia. "I mean, don't they get enough of that at home? This is a party. They need to get with the program."

Matt's parents were also at the party, as well as a few of their adult friends. They were sitting in lawn chairs around a patio table drinking beer and playing cards. They weren't concerned at all with the chaos.

High school kids were running in and out of their house, yelling, screaming and laughing. Loud music was playing, and a few kids were making out in the garage. My parents were lenient, but even this was a bit too much.

Matt's younger siblings also had friends over, so needless to say, this was one of the craziest parties I went to all summer. I wasn't complaining. I had a lot of fun. It was just over-the-top.

Trevor showed up late. I was a little surprised to see him at all since I heard he was on vacation. I wasn't expecting to see him, so when he walked into the backyard I did a double take, then I quickly turned away so he wouldn't see me. God knows I was not prepared for him.

I hated the way I acted around him. I liked him. I was glad to know he liked me, but the thought of actually meeting him drove me crazy. I tried to be myself, but I failed, miserably. Everything I did and said from then on was robotic. I was filled with nervous anxiety and excitement, all mixed with fear. I was a mess and hoped Trevor wouldn't notice.

Because I wasn't expecting to see him, I dressed down. I wore my black faded jeans and a sweatshirt. I mean, who ever wore black jeans? What was I thinking? My mom bought me the jeans and I wanted to make her happy by wearing them. It was a bad night to impress my mom. And what was up with the sweatshirt? I owned so many cute shirts.

I wore very little make-up and my hair was up in a tussle on the top of my head. If there was ever a time I wished I could go back and do it over, this was it. Why didn't I try a little harder to look nice, even if just for myself?

"You look fine." Amelia grumbled at me.

"You look great," Cindy said. "You always look great."

I didn't feel like I looked great. I didn't feel pretty at all. I felt unworthy, self conscious, embarrassed and ugly. I was so discouraged I didn't even notice that Trevor was standing next to me.

"Hello," he said.

"Hello," I said back--number one most awkward moment by far.

"I hear you made the cheer team," Trevor commented.

"Yes I did," I responded.

"It will be nice to have you cheering for our team. You know I'm on the football team, right?" he asked me.

"Yes, I know," I murmured.

All of a sudden I was short on words. My brain wasn't functioning and the right words weren't forming. I wanted to run. I was born anxious, and my heart was beating out of my chest.

Trevor looked great. He always looked nice. He was a very sharp dresser. He wore a pair of relaxed fit blue jeans and a white polo style shirt. He even wore a pair of brown loafers.

Loafers, I thought, *How cute.*

His hair was a light brown color, short, cropped on top and then spiked. His green eyes were penetrating. I never noticed how beautiful his eyes were, but then I'd never seen them this close before.

I heard people talking all around me, but I wasn't hearing anything. I was solely focused on Trevor. It didn't take long to feel better. I mean, once I quit thinking about the way I looked, and started listening to him, everything was okay.

He asked me a few questions about school. Then I asked him some questions about his family, you know the type of small talk two people have when they have absolutely no idea what to say.

He asked me if I wanted to sit down, so we walked over to a patio table near the pool. We sat down across from each other, but I guess the distance was too great, because he came over and set down next to me.

I looked over at Amelia and Cindy to make sure they were okay. We came to the party together and I didn't want them feeling abandoned. They seemed happy. They smiled really big and reassuring, so I turned back around and continued my conversation with Trevor.

"I thought you were on a vacation," I said to him. "I heard you were out of town."

I was warming up a little. He had an easy going personality and I felt more at ease the more we talked. I remembered talking with Curt on the beach and how hard it was to relax around him. It was much easier with Trevor. It felt nice. I had a few butterflies in my stomach, but not too bad. I kind-of liked the strange way I felt.

I could get used to this, I thought.

Trevor told me about the trip he took with his parents to visit relatives. He said he was only there a few days when he just knew he had to get home. I didn't jump to any conclusions by assuming he needed to get home to see me. He really didn't know me yet, nor did he know I'd be at the party. It was a nice thought.

"I knew Matt was having this party," he continued, "and I was told it would be the party of the summer. I just had to get home. My parents put me on a train, and my friend Mark picked me up. And viola, here I am."

"Well, I am glad you made it." I said, trying not to blush. "It's good to finally meet you."

We sat there for a long time talking about nothing. But I didn't care what we talked about. Just being there with him was good enough for me.

The party went on around us and yet I never noticed anyone else. Trevor had a great sense of humor—he made me laugh. A few times we got up and walked around, but we always ended up back at the table. I asked him if he wanted to play a game of croquet, but he laughed at me. I guess it wasn't macho enough.

At one point Matt came over and offered Trevor a beer. Trevor quickly said no. His cheeks turned red and I knew he was embarrassed. I told him I didn't care, but he still refused. I was a little concerned, but not too bad. Remember, drinking a beer didn't make a guy awful, and I wasn't going to worry about nothing.

I saw quite a few kids with beer in their hands. This was the first party I went to that served alcohol. I never drank nor did I plan to, but for some reason I wanted one. I didn't say anything about it. I was driving, so I let it go.

I was afraid of hanging out with people who drank. I never did before. I heard enough stories about peer pressure to know what I was feeling. Maybe I needed to go home.

My mom told me about her girlfriend in high school who drank. She said her friend got drunk at every party she went to, so my mom went with her to keep her safe. She said there was one night her friend went into a room with a guy, and my mom had to literally kick a hole in the door to get the guy to open it.

She warned me that alcohol and teenagers didn't mix, and I was wise to stay far away from it and friends who drank. I could go on and on with the stories I heard. The more I thought about them, the more scared I got.

The story with the biggest impact was the one my mom told me about her college roommate. She said the two of them went to a guy's house—he worked next-door to where they lived. It seemed innocent enough until he put a drug in her friend's drink.

It was hard for her to tell the story because at the time she was young and felt so helpless. They kept her friend in the room for hours and there was nothing she could do. She knew her friend was raped that night—something they never talked about. But the evening had a huge impact on both of them. That's the night my mom decided she would never drink again—and she doesn't.

When I looked at my watch I panicked. Somehow the time got away from me and it was half past one in the morning. My curfew was midnight. I excused myself and ran in the house to call my mom. Luckily no one answered the phone. I quietly left a message and ran back outside to get my friends. I needed to get home before my parents woke up and realized I wasn't there.

"I'm sorry Trevor, it's getting late and I have to go."

It was another awkward moment. I wasn't sure what to do. I wanted to ask him to call me or at least tell me when I'd see him again. I was afraid I'd go home and he wouldn't call.

After a few uncomfortable moments, he stood up, looked into my eyes and said, "Would you like to hang out with me tomorrow night?"

Would I? I thought, *are you kidding?* Then I very politely and quietly said, "Sure that would be nice." I gave him my phone number and went home.

The smile on my face extended from ear to ear all the way home as Amelia and Cindy taunted me, "Honey and Trevor, Honey and Trevor." I was so exited I didn't care what they said.

When I pulled up in front of my house I noticed my parent's car was gone. Then I remembered they went away for the evening. They were not even home. They were not coming home. I could have stayed out all night.

I was frustrated that I forgot they were going away. What was wrong with me? Why didn't I remember? I lost out on spending the entire night with Trevor, and boy was I disappointed.

I was far too worked up to sleep, so I turned on the television and flipped through the channels until about three. I had this funny feeling in my stomach—it was a good feeling, yet I was afraid. What if he didn't call me? What if he got home and decided he didn't like me? What if after talking to me he thought I was boring?

Of course none of that was true. He asked me out after we talked. *He wouldn't have asked me out if he didn't want to go out with me.*

Thoughts raced through my head for hours and then I finally fell asleep. When I awoke I was still on the couch and it was nine o' clock in the morning. I was still exhausted so I went to my room to get a few more hours of sleep. But when I laid down thoughts began racing through my head again. I just kept thinking about the night before.

I replayed our entire conversation over and over again, analyzing every word. I had to make sure I didn't say anything dumb like I did sometimes. At least if I remembered saying something stupid, I'd know the reason why he didn't call—if he didn't call. Was he going to call?

I was driving myself crazy. What happened to the promise I made to never do this again? What happened to my decision that guys weren't worthy of the heartache they caused. I was totally stressed out with no one to blame but myself.

So much for my declaration to stay away from boys; I completely failed the test.

However, I had a bigger concern I needed to address—the alcohol. I think God kept speaking that word to me, because no matter how hard I tried to forget about it, I couldn't.

I had these friends from church who always sat in a circle on the lawn during lunch. I often wished I was a part of their group, yet I didn't fit in. I knew I was different. These girls didn't go to parties. They didn't want to. They were quite content hanging out with each other or going to church events.

We all went to church together—for years. They were my church friends. I loved them like sisters, but I never felt like I was a part of them. Not anymore. Maybe it was my own lack of confidence, maybe guilt, or maybe I was right? I was certain they didn't wake up in the morning concerned about alcohol.

They had a relationship with God I didn't understand. They seemed connected in a way I wasn't. I wanted to go to parties, but why? Why wasn't I content just to hang out and be good? It used to be easy.

God was very real to me—I loved Him. I knew God existed. I never doubted. God, to me, was way up in the heavens too busy to concern Himself with my life. But I did respect Him and tried to be good.

Maybe I lost my way when I joined the cheer team. I heard you can't hang around with a bunch of unbelievers and not be affected by them. But this was a Christian school? I thought everyone here was a believer? Obviously there were different levels of Christian.

TWO STEPS FORWARD THREE STEPS BACK

Every second of every minute of every hour dragged on all morning, and every time the phone rang my stomach hurt. Most of the calls were from my friends who wanted to hear 'all about last night.'

It took Trevor until 2:30 to call me. "Hi Honey," he began. "I'm sorry I didn't call you sooner. I had chores to do. With my parents out of town and all, my dad asked me to do a few things around the house."

"That's okay," I replied. "I was quite busy myself, and I didn't even realize the time."

I lied. I didn't want him thinking I sat by the phone all day waiting for his call. The last thing I wanted was for him to think I was that kind of girl. You know the kind: the type of girl who sits around all day doing nothing, waiting for her guy to call. I saw enough of those relationships on TV to know that was never going to be me.

Even some of my friends on the cheer team complained about boyfriends who didn't respect them enough to call. Even just to say they couldn't talk right now. I was not going to be that type of girl. It wasn't happening.

So I acted aloof. I pretended it didn't matter. But the fact was, it was already 2:30 in the afternoon and our date was in only a few short hours. I mean, what was he thinking?

After I calmed down, we settled into a nice little chat. I told him my parents were out of town and weren't due back for awhile. I asked him if he wanted to come by just to hang out before dinner. He said yes, and we got off the phone.

I already had my outfit picked out. I was definitely not wearing black jeans again. I wore this cute little white dress I picked out earlier that week shopping with my mom. We both saw the dress in the store window at the same time.

"Mom, look at that dress. Isn't it cute?"

"You would look great in that dress," my mom replied. "That is an ideal Honey dress. Let's buy it."

So my mom bought me the dress and I was really glad, because now I had the perfect dress to wear on my first date with Trevor. It was too bad my mom wasn't home to see me leave. Maybe she'd be back when I got home.

I immediately called Amelia to let her know Trevor called. I knew she was waiting and I wanted to call her before she called me. Cindy was visiting with Amelia so I only had to make one phone call. They were both very happy for me.

I had a few new friends on the cheer team to tell, but I didn't have enough time to call them. I decided to wait another day to let them know about my date with Trevor. I was so excited.

"He's on his way over to hang out before dinner," I told Amelia. "We're going to the Red Wren at 6:00 so that gives us a few hours to talk, if he gets here soon. I told him to give me an hour to shower and get ready. I would have showered earlier, but I was afraid I would be in the shower and miss his call."

"Do these guys know their power over us?" I continued. "I think it's awful. We need to change the rules. Girls call the guys and make the plans. At least we would do things right, and never make them wait all day."

Amelia agreed with me. She told me to have a good time, and made me promise to call her first thing in the morning. I promised, and then I jumped in the shower to get ready for my date.

It was my first date. The rules of the house stated we could not date until we were sixteen. I turned seventeen just a few weeks prior but never dated. My sisters were ten and fourteen. Hope, the fourteen-year-old, had more boyfriends than I did. I think she prayed every night that God would speed up time for her so she could date.

I felt sorry for her. Time wasn't going to go any faster. I knew, because I wanted school to be over, and at that time I still had another year. My youngest sister Heather had a long time to go, but she was too young to concern herself with boys. Sometimes I wished I was ten again. Life was so much easier.

I was told that people matured at different speeds. I wasn't concerned about my lack of desire for boyfriends. I was very busy living life doing things I enjoyed. I found a few boys interesting, but was never attracted to them that way. Not like I was now.

Trevor was a little late. I wasn't surprised. After twenty minutes of running to the door every time I heard a car go by, he finally showed up. He drove a dingy blue Toyota Corolla. I think the year of the car was early like maybe a 1978. It looked really old.

When I turned sixteen, my parents bought me a beautiful, brand new, sporty Mustang. I was a little embarrassed for him, so I decided to hide my car. There was no need to crush Trevor's ego before we properly got to know each other. A man needed to feel like a man.

I waited until he neared the door before I opened it. I hoped he didn't see me peering at him through the peep hole. It appeared I was overly anxious, but I was actually just saving him from walking all the way up to the door. I knew how nervous he probably was.

When I opened the door, Trevor looked relieved. "You look beautiful," he said.

"Thank you." I responded. "Come in. I'm the only one home. My parents are still out of town and my sisters aren't here either." *I honestly had no idea where my sisters were. I needed to pay more attention to what my family was doing.*

I walked Trevor out into the backyard, and we sat down on the bench overlooking the pool. We still had an hour, so we talked until it was time to go. The more we talked the more comfortable I was.

The friendship felt right; like one that might last awhile. I wondered if he felt the same way. I mean, we got along really well in such a short amount of time. Didn't that mean longevity?

Red Wren was a hang out for many of our school friends. I was amazed at how many of them showed up while we were eating. If it wasn't a member of the football team then it was one of the cheer team. Friends came by our table constantly for two hours.

I was glad we spent so much time talking earlier, because we had very little time to talk at dinner. By the time we were ready to leave, I'd say the entire school had stopped by to see Trevor and I on a date. Almost as if someone had posted a note. Hmmm, I wondered.

On the ride home we each sat quietly watching the road ahead of us. Every now and then Trevor looked over at me and smiled, and I smiled back. I was really nervous. I was afraid he'd try to kiss me goodnight. After that marvelous kiss from Curt at the beach I couldn't imagine anyone kissing as well, so instead of being excited, I was just plain scared.

Trevor pulled up to my house and got out of the car to walk me to the door, but just as we got near the door my dad walked out.

"Hi dad," I said. "This is my friend Trevor. We just had dinner."

"Nice to meet you," my dad replied. "It's good to see you didn't burn the house down while we were gone."

"Ha, ha dad," I laughed sarcastically. "You're so funny."

I invited Trevor in to meet my mom, but he said he had to get home. I think he was more nervous than he let on. Not expecting to see my dad probably caught him off guard. I didn't blame him for wanting to leave.

I was tired anyway. It had been a long couple of days. I told Trevor I had a good time and he turned around and walked back to his car. It was even okay that I didn't get a goodnight kiss. In fact, I was relieved.

I could hardly wait to show my mom how cute I looked in my new dress.

"Mom," I yelled as I walked into the living room, "where are you?"

"I'm in here Honey."

"Hi mom, I wanted you to see how cute I look."

"Oh Honey," she exclaimed, "You look magnificent. Where'd you go?"

"I had my first date." I answered.

"Really, with who?" my mom asked curiously.

"With Trevor," I replied. "Remember Trevor from the football team? I mentioned him a few months ago when I tried out for cheerleading, the guy in the picture. Well, I met him last night at a party and he asked me out. He took me to Red Wren for a hamburger. It was nice."

I could tell my mom was tired so I said goodnight and kissed her cheek.

"Good night Honey," she said. "I'm glad you had a good time. Sorry I wasn't here to help you get ready. Hopefully I'll be around next time. Sleep well."

I went to my room and closed the door. I fell right to sleep.

The next morning my dad came in early to wake me up. "Honey, get up. You'll be late for summer camp if you don't get up now."

"What?" I cried. "What do you mean summer camp? Why didn't you remind me?" I was so caught up with what was going on with Trevor I completely forgot about camp.

I wanted to go, but not now. I just met a boy. I just had my first date. I couldn't leave for a week. No, that wasn't possible.

"Dad I can't go to camp today, not today. You don't understand. I can't go to camp."

"You have to go to camp," My dad exclaimed. "This trip's already paid for and you're going. I'm sorry, but you don't have a choice. Now get up and get ready."

How did I forget about camp? I went every year. I knew about camp for months. How did I forget? What about Amelia? I promised to call her and tell her all about my date. *I'll call her from the bus on my cell phone.*

Oh, but what about Trevor. I had so many things to do. I couldn't go away for a week. Camp came at such a bad time. What was I going to do?

To make it all worse, when I got on the bus, they told me cell phones were not allowed. I had to leave my phone with my dad. I was in shock. Not only was I leaving for a week, I couldn't call anybody. Sure, the camp had pay phones, but all of my phone numbers were programmed in my phone. I never memorized the numbers. I never needed to, not even Amelia's.

I was ruined. I just knew it. All of my friends, especially Trevor, would go on all week without me. Trevor would get tired of waiting, and my friends would feel abandoned. I was devastated. I went to the back of the bus, put my head down and cried.

After my little pity party I looked around to see who else was going to camp. I saw quite a few kids from Sunday school, and a few friends I knew from school, but none that I hung around with. Aubrey, a girl I hung out with every year at camp, was sitting right in front of me. "Hi Aubrey," I said. "I'm so glad you're here. What a nice surprise."

I was especially glad to see her. *Maybe it won't be so bad.*

Bus trips to summer camp took forever. I often wondered why we always traveled so far. Weren't there any mountains or lakes near where we lived? Every year since fourth grade we'd board a bus and set out on a journey faraway. We seldom went to the same place twice. Every campsite was great. I always had a good time. In fact, I cried every year when it was time to leave.

This was my last year at camp, unless I signed up to be a camp counselor, but a counselor was not the same as being a kid at camp. I never envied the counselors. They worked very hard to keep us kids in line. I mean, we were supposed to be good little Christian kids, but we always behaved horribly.

As I sat there thinking, I remembered camp the summer before ninth grade. There was a boy at camp that year by the name of Brett who definitely had his sights on me. Brett was the type of guy you wanted to take home to meet your parents. He was kind, polite, definitely in love with God, but he wasn't my type.

After that summer we wrote each other for awhile, but the spark quickly faded and our relationship ended.

Wow, Brett. I hadn't thought about him in years.

I wonder if he'll be at camp this year.

REMEMBERING WHEN

Before I knew it I was lost in the thoughts of summer camp three years prior. I remembered Brett clearly. He had a charming personality. He was very outgoing and socialized well with everyone. I, on the other hand, didn't socialize well with anyone.

That was an awkward year for me. I was only fourteen, but I matured quickly. I noticed boys staring at me a lot and it was uncomfortable

At that time my heart was set on spending a very relaxing week getting closer to God. At fourteen meeting a boy was definitely not on my list of things to do. But Brett's agenda was different. I could not get away from him all week. That week came back to me as if it were yesterday.

By ninth grade I was in my second year of charter school so I was only in an actual school for a year. By that summer I was happy to be in a cabin with all of my friends from Sunday school—they were the friends I was comfortable with, and I missed them.

At home I was a little more popular than they were, but at camp, we were all equal. I never thought of myself as better than my church friends. In fact, sometimes I envied their simple lives.

It seemed no matter where they went or what they did, they always had a good time. They never complicated things. I wanted to be like that. I wanted to be as simple that week as possible. I just wanted to get along well with others. I wanted to fit in.

After we claimed our cots and unpacked our suitcases, we went out to the parking lot to watch the other buses arrive. Dinner wasn't for another three hours and there wasn't much yet to do. This campsite seemed a little more barren than others. I remembered seeing a pool, but that was about it.

A few buses arrived while we were hanging out. It was fun to see who showed up from the years prior. There were a few girls I recognized who said hi, but not too many. I didn't make friends easily and although a lot of them looked familiar, I never met most of them.

One bus came from an area near where my aunt Stacey and my grandma lived-- about two hours away from my house. When I was younger I used to visit my relatives a lot, but as I got older, and more involved in school, and with my friends, I visited them a lot less. My parents still went often, but I hadn't seen them for about 6 months.

Kids were running off buses. A few fell over their bags. It was a wonder any of them could walk at all with all that stuff. We always brought so much to camp: sleeping bags, pillows, suit cases. They didn't provide anything but toilet paper and food, so we had to bring our own soap and shampoo, stuff like that.

It was about that time Brett got off a bus. He was about 5'7", not too tall, but taller than I was. He had shoulder length, curly brown hair. He was slender, and he was cute. He kept calling after his friend, "Kirk, wait up." He didn't seem to notice me or anyone else standing there. He just kept walking.

How interesting, I thought.

He intrigued me right away. He had a certain attractive confidence about him. I could tell he liked himself. I often wished I had more confidence. I didn't like myself much at all.

I was the type of person who ran from people I saw, because I knew they didn't want to see me. My mom said I was crazy. She told me to talk to them. She said I might be surprised. I don't know why I always assumed people hated me. I don't know why I was so insecure.

I was home-schooled for such a long time and really had very little interaction with people. Maybe that was it. I know I felt comfortable with some people, but ran away from most everybody else. I could tell Brett probably talked to everyone.

It wasn't until dinner that Brett first noticed me. Aubrey and I went into the cafeteria early since we had nothing else to do. They wouldn't serve us, but they did let us sit inside to wait.

About twenty minutes later Brett came into the cafeteria to ask what time dinner was. A food worker told him he had to wait. That's when he turned and saw us. "Well, what about them," he asked. "Do they get to eat already?"

"We're not eating," I said. "We're waiting."

Brett walked over to our table and sat down. Aubrey was embarrassed and started blushing. I acted disinterested. I really didn't like boys, although inwardly, I was jumping with excitement. This was all very new for me. Remember, I was only fourteen.

"I'll just sit here too and wait," he said. "Do you mind?"

I hesitated a few moments. I had to think about it. Here was a fascinating guy wanting to sit with Aubrey and me, and even though I was curious, that was really the last thing I wanted. I was so confused.

Even though everything within me was shouting, *say no,* I kindly smiled at Brett and replied, "Sure, you can join us."

Brett told us his name. He mentioned he was from Porterville. He told us his church was the Living Water Christian Fellowship.

"That's my aunt Stacey's church," I shouted. "Do you know Stacey Caruthers?"

I attended church with my aunt Stacey a few times before, but she only recently started going to Living Water. However, I did remember seeing Brett at their Christmas party. I probably wasn't very interested in him, because I only remembered him vaguely.

"I do know Stacey and her husband Steve," Brett replied. "They are good friends with my parents. Do you live there too?"

All of a sudden Brett seemed interested. A little too interested in my opinion.

"No. I don't live near you. I live two hours away in a city near Los Angeles. I went to your church once before though, and I even think I saw you last year at a Christmas party."

That was the wrong thing to say. Brett sat up in his chair and began talking. He talked as if he had known me for years. He talked about anything and everything. I thought he was never going to stop. Aubrey and I looked at each other and laughed. We had a new friend.

When it was time for dinner, they opened the doors, and kids came pouring into the cafeteria. Brett was so busy talking he didn't notice.

"Brett," I interrupted, "if we don't get into line we won't get any food. It'll all be gone."

Quickly we jumped up and ran into line, and Brett just kept on talking.

27

After dinner there was a worship service. We had a few minutes before it started, so we went back to our cabins to clean up. I brushed my teeth and changed from my shorts into long pants. The days were hot, but the air grew cold at night. I grabbed my sweatshirt and my Bible, and Aubrey and I headed over to the fellowship hall. It was near a lake. "Hey Aubrey, look, there's a lake," I shouted.

It was a beautiful night. I thought about how nice it would be sitting in a boat on the lake. There was a slight breeze and the tall trees were swaying. The sun was setting beyond the lake and the reflection on the water was spectacular.

Aubrey and I went inside the hall and sat near the back. I always sat near the back. After I sat down I could see Brett sitting near the front. I was glad. He was a nice boy, but I didn't come to camp to meet a boy. And I knew I couldn't take anymore of his talking.

Sitting in the back, far away from him, was perfect, until he saw me. I turned my head quickly, trying to hide from his view, but it was too late. Within seconds he was sitting next to me. When I turned to look at Aubrey she was shaking her head and laughing.

The worship service lasted almost two hours. We started off singing praise songs to God. Worship was my favorite part of church and we always sang the best songs at camp.

I loved to sing loud, even though I didn't sing well, but it was hard singing loud sitting next to Brett. I felt self conscious and hindered. But surprisingly when I looked over at Brett, he was singing with his eyes closed and his hands lifted up.

Wow, I thought to myself. *How impressive is that?*

I came from a conservative church, but there were members who raised their hands. We always clapped during upbeat songs, and that wasn't a problem for me, but raising my hands was hard.

I noticed how easy it was for Brett. He seemed lost in the songs, almost as if he was privately communicating with God. I envied him. I wished I had the confidence to raise my hands to God, but I always thought everyone was looking at me. How vain was that.

The guest speaker was the best speaker I ever heard. But I said that every year. I didn't know who chose the camp speakers, but they were always encouraging. Their messages always spoke to me personally about subjects relevant to my life. Every year I wished my pastors could speak as well. Maybe then I would want to go to church.

This speaker taught about the Holy Spirit and he immediately had my attention. We didn't talk much about Him in my youth group so I was quite ignorant. He talked about being filled with the Holy Spirit for empowerment to live a victorious life.

I tapped Aubrey on the shoulder and quietly said, "I could sure use some of that." She smiled back at me and nodded.

Brett seemed especially interested. He definitely knew what the preacher was talking about. By the end of the service I found myself extremely fascinated by Brett's obvious love for God. It was truly inspiring.

Although I loved God, and spent most of my life learning about God, I definitely did not have the same relationship with God that I saw in Brett. I was also a little surprised that in all the conversation we had earlier in the day he never one time talked about God. Maybe he just assumed since we were at a church camp that we were both on the same spiritual page.

After the worship service Brett walked Aubrey and I back to our cabin. It was getting late and camp curfew was strictly enforced. The girls stayed in cabins on one side of the camp, and the boys slept in teepees on the other.

The girls had a much better deal. We had cabins with windows and doors. The teepees had no security. I envisioned bears or other wild animals entering the teepees while the boys were sleeping. I was glad we had four walls made of wood.

Brett didn't hang around. He said goodbye and went to his side of the camp. I was glad, but a little disappointed. Something about his relationship with God sparked my interest, and surprisingly I hoped he might stay around and talk some more. We didn't talk at all about God and I thought maybe he might shed some light on the message.

Don't worry Honey, I thought. *You have an entire week to get to know him.*

I went inside the cabin, curled up in my sleeping bag, and went to sleep. I dreamt about Brett all night.

Interesting, I thought.

BACK TO REALITY

The mornings in the mountains were the best. When I awoke that first morning I was reminded how much I loved the mountain morning air. It was difficult to describe when asked what I meant about the scent. I always said the same thing, "It smells like cold mixed with trees."

The smell of pine when it was cold was clearly described by only one word, *refreshing*. I told my mom, "Better felt than telt. You just need to experience it for yourself."

There were hundreds of birds living in the trees there on the hill. The sound was amazing. I can't remember too many birds chirping in Los Angeles. I think all the birds lived here in the mountains. I woke up extra early at camp just to take in the beauty of the surroundings. It was easier to find quiet time in the morning, and the silence always drew me closer to God.

Every year brought the same hope. I spent a week at camp focused on nothing but God and nature. I got to know God better than I had all year, and then I got on a bus, went down the mountain and forget all about Him.

Every year I vowed to return home a different person, and this year was no exception. I got reborn. I turned into the new creature the Bible talked about, and I wanted this year to be different.

As I sat on the rock outside my cabin, I wondered, *how will I make this year different? How will I make this the year of permanent transformation? How will I change and stay changed?*

While taking in all the beautiful sights, smells and sounds of camp, Aubrey came out to join me. We sat there quietly until breakfast and then headed down the mountain to the cafeteria.

Most of my camp friends hated camp food, but I loved it. Powdered eggs never bothered me. Mondays were always the best. Every year on Monday morning they served pancakes with strawberries and whipped cream. I was an extremely thin ninth grader and I could eat as many pancakes dripping in strawberry syrup as I wanted.

I was also an active runner. My dad told me I ran like a deer. Because I liked to run, and I ran well, I stayed thin. I did tend to overeat, but compensated extra eating with lots of exercise. This week was no exception.

Everyday the camp planned some type of physical activity. There were tag races through the orchard, water sports in the pool, relay races down a water slide, horseback riding, and lake swimming events. I participated in every activity and won them all too, except for the races against the boys.

Brett and his friend Kirk were also very athletic. As hard as I tried I couldn't beat them. Brett obviously enjoyed the competitions; especially the games against me. The more Brett and I did together the more intrigued I was.

My first impression of camp was completely wrong. There was more going on this year than ever before. There was a constant flow of games and activities—never a dull moment. During free time they opened the doors to the recreation room filled with arcade and computer games.

The only rule was no TV and no internet. They wanted us to spend the week getting closer to God and to each other. The supervisors knew spending time on the internet, or using cell phones, would defeat the purpose of our week away from the outside world.

Not only was my first impression of camp wrong, my first impression of Brett was wrong too. Sure he talked a lot, but he was also quietly passionate. He was alive and on fire for God.

I had grandparents who preached in a Charismatic church who loved God more than anyone I knew. I saw Jesus in my grandparents. Brett portrayed the same Godly character I saw in them. I saw Jesus in Brett, and it was amazing. The more time I spent with Brett the more time I wanted to spend with God. I wondered if he knew how contagious his love for God was.

Of course he does. If I knew God the way Brett does, I would surely know.

Maybe if I get really close, his passion will rub off on me. Maybe if I spend all week with Brett I can go home the changed person I desired.

The second night at camp, after the evening worship service, Brett asked me to take a walk with him. He said he wanted to talk in private for awhile and with Aubrey and Kirk around all the time he said privacy was hard to find.

He talked me into taking off my camp bracelet and crossing over into forbidden territory. He said we could walk down the mountain, and without our bracelets on, no one would know we didn't belong there.

What did I know? I was barely in the ninth grade and very vulnerable. I took off my bracelet and walked down the mountain away from camp, alone with Brett. At first I was scared. I wasn't a rebel and seldom got into trouble. But after a few minutes I relaxed. It was exciting.

Brett still didn't talk a lot about God. He talked more about himself. You know: sports, jobs, his parents, places he'd been. Brett knew how to talk. I didn't like talking. I was an introvert. Brett carried the conversation, so whenever Brett stopped talking, the conversation died.

About ten minutes into the walk Brett grabbed my hand. It was nice. I was a little afraid of what he might try to do next, but nothing else ever happened. He was a perfect gentleman. At fifteen years of age, I hoped so.

After about thirty minutes I grew restless, and I feared getting caught. I don't know why I didn't think of it earlier, but all of a sudden the thought crossed my mind, *wouldn't our counselors wonder where we were?*

Panic set in and I shouted, "Brett, let's go back. We're going to get into trouble."

"Calm down Honey," Brett replied. "Everything is all right."

We turned around and quickly headed back towards camp, but it was too late. I was right. The counselors were looking for us, and we were in a lot of trouble. They took us into the administration office and told us we were going home. They said we'd be on a bus first thing in the morning.

"We'd put you on a bus right now if it weren't so late," my counselor said. "Go back to your cabins and we will deal with you in the morning."

I looked over at Brett, and he just winked at me. I wasn't amused.

I quietly turned around and went back to my cabin. When I walked in everyone stared at me. "I'm sorry," I said, "I didn't mean to worry any of you."

I spent a few minutes brushing my teeth and washing my face, and then I curled up in my sleeping bag and went to sleep. Before I fell asleep I quietly prayed, "Dear God, please don't let them send me home."

Well God heard my prayer and had mercy on me because when I woke up the next morning the counselors had changed their minds. They gave us a warning and made us promise to never leave the camp again. They said something about a liability. I was relieved. I was terrified they would call my parents.

Only one other time in my life was I that scared. It was in summer school before the eighth grade. I was taking a metal shop class with a bunch of boys. There were only two girls in the class, Denise and I. I knew from day one that the teacher did not like me. He was very male chauvinistic and disliked girls in his metal shop class.

I disagreed with him. My mom had taken wood shop at the adult school and made some very nice shelves for the bathroom. I wanted to make something pretty too, and this was my chance. After a few weeks into the class my project was finished and instead of starting another one I sat around and watched the other students make their projects.

The teacher didn't like that I had nothing to do, so he asked me to leave his class. I told him he was acting ridiculous, so he sent me to the principal's office. He told him I was being flippant and rude, but I was no such thing. The principal called my parents and I was sent home.

Before my parents came for me the principal allowed me to tell my mom over the phone what happened, but I couldn't talk. I was too afraid. My throat swelled up and I couldn't speak. Lucky for me the principal told my parents he had trouble with this teacher before so I wasn't in any real trouble, but I did have to un-enroll from the class.

The situation was definitely unfair, but I did learn a lesson. My first year in a real school, I enrolled in home economics where I learned how to sew clothes and make food. It was a much better choice.

Brett felt bad. I could see it all over his face. He looked as if his dog had just run away.

"Honey," he started, "I am so sorry I got you in trouble. I never meant for that to happen. I hope you can forgive me and give me another chance. I promise I won't coerce you into doing anything else wrong, not now, not ever. What do you say?"

I thought it was sweet he cared so much, but he really didn't need to grovel. I wasn't planning on shunning him the rest of the week over a minor incident. I knew he meant no harm.

"It's okay Brett," I replied. "You're forgiven."

There were a few close calls during the remaining days at camp, but nothing too serious. Brett needed to be alone with me and it was obvious he was going to do whatever it took.

This was the first time a boy was ever interested in me in that way. Brett was everywhere I was for a week. Every time I turned around he was there. Most boys that age hid their feelings. Brett was one boy who had no intentions of hiding his feelings for me, and I liked it.

Of course I played hard to get. I didn't know how to express myself. I had never had a guy friend before, and I didn't know how to be a girlfriend. But Brett didn't mind. He hung around anyway. He was my first real experience of what love might be like and I appreciated it.

By the end of the week I had made a few new friends. Leaving them was hard, as it was every year. Aubrey was someone I saw every Sunday at church, but not someone I hung out with during the week. I wasn't sure why though, since she was one of the nicest people I knew.

I also met a few other girls from different churches. I exchanged addresses and phone numbers with them. We wrote back and forth for quite awhile, but life got busy and the writing stopped.

Brett was the one I thought I'd keep in touch with forever. He was an amazing person and I was glad to know him. He taught me things I didn't know about God, and I was grateful for the time we spent together.

I was certain to visit aunt Stacey more often so I could see Brett again, but it never happened. That summer my family went on a few vacations, and we never made it to Porterville. Once school started it was near impossible to go anywhere. My sisters and I had extracurricular activities every weekend.

Occasionally my aunt Stacey called to let me know Brett was asking about me. She said he was a great kid and hoped I'd be with a guy like him someday. But over time Brett started dating a local girl and aunt Stacy stopped mentioning him.

I admit in the beginning I was sad he went away, although I knew in my heart it was best for him. I was happy for him, but guys like Brett didn't come around everyday and I knew his friendship would be hard to replace.

This was the first time, in a long time, that I thought about Brett. He never made it to camp the following two years, and I wondered if he was coming this year.

The spiritual impact Brett made on my life was huge, but just as always, I went down the mountain and forgot all about it. This was the first time in years I remembered that summer and what it was like to have feelings for a boy and to fall in love with God.

SIMPLY COMPLICATED

Reminiscing about the past took my mind off of leaving my friends and Trevor for a week, and not saying goodbye. Wondering if Brett would be at camp was exciting.

Aubrey startled me when she tapped me on the shoulder. "Honey," she whispered, "I'm so glad we get to spend another week at camp together. It's too bad it'll be our last. I wonder if Brett will show up."

I just smiled and shrugged my shoulders. I shook my head as if to say, *I wonder too*. She had no idea I just spent the last few hours wondering that very same thing.

The last hour seemed to take the longest. The mountain road was very windy, so the bus had to go especially slow. I wasn't fond of windy mountain roads so I kept my eyes closed while we were on them. Occasionally I peeked out to see where we were. It was amazing how beautiful it was up there on that mountain.

I was told that Pine Lake was spectacular. Whoever told me that was right. It was truly remarkable. The whole camp was situated on top of a rolling hill so nothing was built on flatland, except the pool of course.

Every cabin and every building was built along windy roads leading up and down mountainsides. Down at the bottom of the hill was a beautiful pool and across the path was Pine Lake. The lake was as blue as the sky.

I pictured myself sitting in a boat on the lake with Trevor, enjoying a romantic afternoon like I saw in the movies. The girls wore those big straw hats and fancy frilly dresses, and it always seemed strange why they got all dressed up just to sit in a boat on a lake.

What if the boat tipped over and the girl got all wet; her fancy outfit ruined. I just never understood. But now that I was thinking about my own romantic encounter, the frilly dress and big straw hat seemed quite the appropriate outfit to wear.

I was greatly relieved when the bus came to a stop. Since I sat in the back I waited until the other kids got off. Aubrey and I stood up together, gathered our stuff, and headed towards the door. It all felt so familiar. Every year, since the fourth grade, it was the same thing. We climbed off a bus with arms full of luggage, a sleeping bag and pillow, and walked to some cabin to unload.

But somehow this year felt different. Maybe because it was my last year; maybe because I was older; maybe because I just met a boy; or maybe because I just made the cheerleading team. Whatever the reason, one thing was perfectly clear, God was the farthest thing from my mind, and that was a problem.

Here I was one more time up on a mountain at camp ready to spend an entire week worshiping and praising God, the same God I vowed to get closer to every year, and I was still no closer to Him than I was the previous year. Maybe I needed to give up all hope of ever changing.

Whatever the reason for my melancholy mood, and God knew there were plenty, Aubrey noticed. "Honey, what's wrong? You look as if you're going to cry."

I was sad. My life down the mountain in the city was just ordinary, and I knew that. Most of the time I did what came next with no thought to what I was doing. My life was just like that.

Of course there were exceptions, like trying out for cheerleading and meeting boys. But even those experiences didn't elevate me to a higher place. They just kind of happened—no big deal.

34

Establishing a relationship with God proved to be a challenge. For some reason it did not come naturally. Even after the wonderful week I spent at camp with Brett, my enthusiasm for God didn't last longer than a few weeks. That was the year I was certain to go down the mountain permanently changed, but I didn't. I never did.

Sure, for a few weeks after camp I glowed like a torch, but somehow the fire always went out, and I was right back into my old routine, God on Sundays and sometimes on Wednesdays.

I never gave it too much thought until I saw how much Brett loved God. That was the year my eyes were opened to the fact that one could actually know God on a much deeper level.

But now that I knew someone whose relationship with God was on the same level as a best friend, I accepted that would never be me. In fact, my only hope was to get through the week without wanting to go home.

I needed to find enough things to do to keep busy. Leaving Trevor and all my friends made me think this would be the longest week of my life. Fortunately after only a few minutes my outlook changed.

It was probably the third bus that rolled in after our bus arrived. I was already headed up the hill towards my cabin when I heard him call my name, "Honey Sweetheart, is that you?"

Even after all that time on the bus thinking about the great time I had with Brett three years prior, and pondering how much I wanted to see him again, nothing prepared me for the way I felt when I heard his voice. I recognized it as him as soon as I heard my name.

I turned around and Brett was standing there. There are no words to describe how I felt. I put my stuff on a rock, and ran down the hill as fast as I could. I jumped into his arms and he held me forever. As much as I wanted him to be there, I was still very surprised. I had no way of knowing if he was coming or not.

This was better than a hot fudge sundae, I said to myself. *Seeing Brett was even better than making the cheerleading team.* But I was puzzled. *If I am this happy to see him, then why did we not stay in touch?*

Brett was as happy to see me as I was him. He had me wait while he got his things and then we walked up the hill together. Aubrey had already gone to the cabin, so I felt comfortable walking with Brett.

Aubrey was a very understanding person. She never cared when I spent time with other people. She wasn't needy. I liked that about her. She was my best friend at camp and I appreciated her. I hoped she knew that.

Again I wondered, *why don't I spend time with Aubrey at home?*

Our cabins were located across the camp from each other—quite a distance. Of course the girl's cabins were not near the boy's. That was best for a bunch of high school kids with hormone levels at their highest.

After Brett dropped me off at my cabin, before he went on to his, he told me how good it was to see me. He told me he thought about me often and hoped I would be here. He apologized for not keeping in touch, as did I, and assured me he'd do a much better job after this week.

He seemed a little quieter, much more mature. I think we both grew up. We were quieter, calmer and a bit more reserved, although I know I was quieter at camp than I was at home. My sisters still called me squirrelly, even after I turned seventeen, but out in public I was different.

I was high-strung and hyperactive around Amelia and Cindy, but so were they—we brought that out of each other. Around the cheer team I acted more mature. I knew how to behave according to whom I was around. Didn't everyone?

Brett was definitely better looking this year. His hair was a bit shorter, and he was at least three inches taller. He was still slim and very attractive. He had a huge bright smile—just as I remembered.

One reason I admired Brett was how he radiated with the love of God. This year was no exception. In fact, if you ask me, he glowed even more. I actually saw Jesus more in Brett this year than I did in ninth grade, and I was convinced at that time, nobody loved God more than he did.

Now I felt even worse about my relationship with God. Not only was I a total failure at knowing God, Brett obviously knew him better now than he did before. *What was I missing?*

Although seeing Brett again was exciting, I was well aware of my new boyfriend back at home. When I first met Brett there wasn't anyone else. I didn't have a boyfriend at fourteen. I was not allowed to date until I turned sixteen. This year, although definitely still intrigued by Brett, Trevor was now in the picture. I knew the potential complication of the situation, and I had no idea what to do.

After I made my bed and put my things away, I went to the recreation room to call my mom. I told her to tell all of my friends where I was and when I'd be home. I asked my mom to have Amelia track down Trevor. I needed her to explain to him what happened. I didn't want him getting the wrong impression, and I knew after a week he would wonder.

I took a little time after talking to my mom to seek God about the situation. I told Him I was confused and asked Him to help me. I told Him I needed His direction in order to make wise decisions. I shared with God my struggle and asked Him to show me His way. I was so tired of my own way.

Seeing Brett again brought up a whole bunch of old feelings. I spent the last three years pushing him out of my mind. And as much as I hoped to see him I was now faced with a terrible dilemma.

I told God if He wanted me with Brett he needed to change me. I asked God to help me understand Him more. I wanted to choose the right way and not the wrong way, yet I didn't know how. I knew Trevor wasn't right for me. Deep inside my soul I knew Trevor was wrong. But I didn't know any other way.

I remembered hearing a message on God's transforming power. I knew God could change me. I asked Him to take the week to transform me into a better person. I wanted to be more like Brett.

This year Brett didn't spend all of his time with me. He sat with me occasionally during the church services, but he never sat with me during meals. He came to camp with a group of guys and he hung around with them most of the week, except for the evenings. He always hooked up with me after the last service right before lights out.

Each night we sat near my cabin and talked. He never suggested leaving the area. I guess he learned his lesson from our ninth grade catastrophe. We talked about everything. This year he talked a lot about God. He told me he was pursuing a career in the ministry. He said he decided to devote his entire life to God.

"That is so wonderful," I replied. "I wish I was that dedicated."

I shared with Brett how hard it was for me to connect with God. I told him how difficult it was to keep God first. I sensed he didn't understand because he looked very confused. I suppose because he loved God so deeply, he thought that I should too.

I tried to share how I felt in a way that made sense, but he didn't understand. He wanted so badly to believe I was the girl God chose for him, yet I knew in my heart I was not.

Aubrey and I got up extra early to jog around the lake. There was a dirt path that ran through the trees along the water. It was quite a few miles, so we got up early and jogged fast. On those days when we ran slowly, we ate late.

The cafeteria stayed open for a little while after breakfast. They offered muffins, fruit and juice for those who slept in. So on those mornings when we lagged there was always something to eat.

I appreciated the system. None of the other camps I attended allowed campers to eat anytime they wanted. There was usually one breakfast time, and if you didn't make it, you didn't eat.

This year I spent a lot of time lying out by the pool and visiting friends in the social hall. Every year I participated in most of the camp activities, but this year I wanted to relax. I did a whole lot of nothing, and I enjoyed every minute.

On the last day of camp, dinner turned into a banquet, and the boys asked the girls for a date. Of course Brett asked me early in the week. I think he feared if he didn't grab me quickly, someone else would. I said yes.

There wasn't anyone else at camp I cared to attend the banquet with, but I was afraid if some other guy asked me I'd feel obligated to say yes. I hated saying no. Brett was the best looking guy there and all the other girls were jealous. I tried not to boast, but I was definitely delighted.

The banquet required a little more than casual dress. I brought a nicer pair of pants and a cute pink shirt my mom made for me. I let Aubrey curl my hair, and I put on a little makeup.

I never wore makeup at camp. I saw no reason to. Every time I went swimming I'd have mascara running down my face and I didn't see the point. But the banquet was a special occasion calling for a little eye shadow.

A few minutes before dinner, Brett came to get me. We walked to the cafeteria arm in arm. It was quite romantic. Brett also wore a nicer looking shirt, although he still wore his jeans. Most of the kids didn't know about the banquet, so they were not prepared. I remembered reading about it in the camp brochure. I guess Brett read about it too.

The tables were decorated with candles and flowers. There were water glasses and pitchers sitting around fancy centerpieces. There were baskets of rolls with butter, and ceramic dishes filled with mints. It felt like a real date.

Brett pulled out my chair and I sat down, then he sat down next to me. I looked over at him and smiled. He leaned over and kissed my cheek. Butterflies danced in my stomach, and I knew I was in trouble.

At the end of the banquet, the guest speaker spoke a little about the week at camp and the different sermons. He elaborated on living the life of Christ and striving to be more like Jesus.

He told us of the importance of evangelism. He encouraged us to go out into our communities to tell others about Jesus. He challenged those in the group, the ones who committed their lives to God, to stand up. Brett stood up, but I just sat there.

I didn't know exactly how many kids attended camp that summer, but I saw how many stood up. Only five kids stood up when asked to commit their lives to Christ. Only five kids had the same deep love for God that Brett had. How sad was that?

At the time I was relieved. There were far more kids sitting than standing, and I wasn't standing. Blending in with the majority was easier than trying to hide from them. But looking back I am sad that more of the youth did not know God. I am sad that knowing God was so difficult.

In my opinion, knowing God on a deeper level was like trying to find one star in a billion, when the one star was hiding behind a cloud. And it was obvious; I wasn't the only one who couldn't find it.

On the morning we were to return home, Brett came to my cabin early. He wanted to see as much of me as possible before leaving. We talked about the future, and I finally mentioned Trevor, but he ignored me.

He said he'd call and make plans to go out. He said that living two hours away wasn't a problem now that we both drove. He asked me if we could go to the beach while it was still hot. I said maybe.

I was sad saying goodbye. I was always sad saying goodbye. It didn't matter who it was; my friends, relatives or casual acquaintances, when I said goodbye, I cried.

Like always I had met a few new people and after we exchanged phone numbers we promised to call and write. But I knew it wouldn't last. It never did. I guess that's why I was sad. I knew a day would come when the texting would stop and the friendships would cease. It happened that way every year.

As hard as it was leaving camp for the very last time, I was also excited about going home. I had a great week, much better than expected, but I was definitely ready to see all of my friends, especially Trevor.

Spending the week with Brett was wonderful, but I was concerned. I really wasn't the right girl for him. He deserved someone so much better—a girl who loved God like he did.

A transformation did not happen in me and I couldn't make the commitment. I couldn't even if I wanted to. I had no idea how. So I thanked Brett for a wonderful week and told him to give me a call.

"Maybe we can get together," I said.

Aubrey and I headed towards the back of the bus. Waving goodbye we wiped the tears from our eyes and sat down. We each took our own row so we could stretch out. We were both exhausted and looked forward to a long nap.

It seemed like I had just closed my eyes when Aubrey shook me. "Wake up Honey, we're home." I looked out the window and saw my mom. I was so glad to see her.

WHAT A MESS

I couldn't wait to check my messages. I was anxious to see if Trevor had called. "Mom, do you have my cell phone?"

"The phone is at the house," my mom replied. "I'm sorry I didn't bring it."

"That's okay," I said. "I'll call my friends when I get home."

I was a little disappointed, but we lived close to the church, so I knew we'd be there soon. Listening to my messages at home in private was better anyway. If Trevor called I might scream. If he didn't, I might cry. Alone in my room was the best place either way. As soon as we pulled into the driveway, I ran into the house, grabbed my phone, and ran to my room. But the phone was dead.

"No," I shouted. "This can't be happening." I kicked the door shut.

Only four hours down the mountain, and there I was back to my old self. Only a few hours away from peace and serenity, and I was already angry and yelling.

See Honey, I said to myself. *You are a total failure. Brett is so much better off without you.*

I found the charger and plugged in my phone. I took a shower first to calm down. I was so uptight. I wondered why I exploded so easily. *Was I mentally defective? Was it a food allergy? Did my mom drop me on my head at birth?* If only I could think before reacting.

My phone only held eight messages, but I could see there were quite a few missed calls. I curled up on my bed and listened to the messages, one at a time, but none were from Trevor. *How could that be?* I wondered.

When I searched through the missed calls I saw that he had called four times, but never left a message. *How was I to know how he felt if he didn't leave a message? Maybe he couldn't. Maybe the mailbox was full.*

Next I called Amelia. "Hi Amelia, I'm home. What are you up to?"

"I'm not up to much. Just sitting here bored. Cindy went away for the week and you were gone too. That left me with no one to hang out with and nothing to do. I mean, you are my only two friends."

"Nonsense," I said. "You have lots of friends."

I named several people from school Amelia hung out with. With each name she responded, "She's your friend."

"Whatever," I said. "I'm home now. What do you want to do?"

I really didn't want to hang out with Amelia. I wanted to find out about Trevor. But I felt obligated. Friends never appreciated when other friends put a boyfriend first.

Amelia was very sensitive. Far more sensitive than I was. It was hard for her when I joined the cheer team and made new friends. A boyfriend right now would only add salt to her wound.

I decided to wait until after we were out before asking about Trevor. Actually, I was hoping she would mention him first. I mean, I did ask her to contact him for me. She knew Trevor and I went out on a date. I told her I was interested in him, but I knew Amelia well. As much as I wanted to talk about Trevor I knew that would upset her.

Spending time with Amelia first said I cared about her feelings. Caring about her said a lot about our friendship. I was trying to be thoughtful. Choosing to spend time with a boyfriend or even talking about one, after being away for a week, wasn't the best choice. I knew that.

"How about we go see a movie?" she replied. "It's hot outside and the theatre will be nice and cool."

"Sounds good," I responded. "I'll be over in a few minutes and we'll decide what to see."

After I got off the phone I blew my hair dry and got ready to go. My mom was disappointed that she had to wait to hear about my week, but I promised to come home early and tell her all about it.

As I walked out the door, I thought about how glad I was to be home. I did not like being away for long periods of time, and this year especially, I really missed my friends.

The theatre was located in our big Town Center Mall. We chose a movie that started late, so we had time to walk around. I saw quite a few of my friends there. They all came running over to ask me where I went. I was flattered that they all missed me, but they acted as if I had been gone forever.

"I went to summer camp," I replied. "I go every year with my church. This year was my last year, and I had a great time, but I'm sure glad to be home."

I was surprised to see so many of my friends at the mall but not Trevor. I mean, where was he? I didn't mention him to anyone and no one mentioned him to me. Nobody was offering any information and I wasn't going to ask.

I was tired, even tough I napped on the bus. I didn't feel much like talking, so I was glad when the movie started, so I could hide in the theatre. After the movie I took Amelia home and then went on to my own house. Unfortunately, I got back too late to see my mom. She was already asleep. *I'll tell her about my week in the morning.*

I put on my pajamas, brushed my teeth and crawled into bed. I was so glad to be home sleeping in my own bed again. I slept till after ten. I wanted to sleep longer, but my sisters were downstairs talking on their phones and watching TV--very loudly. I jumped out of bed, ran down the stairs and started yelling, "People are sleeping in this house. Do you mind?"

"Go back to camp," Hope shouted. "We liked it better when you were away."

I woke up cranky and tired and very distraught over Trevor. I wasn't feeling very friendly so I stayed in my room for awhile. Hope was right. I liked me better too when I was away.

Why do I act like this? I thought. *Why can't I communicate without yelling?*

For a whole week I never raised my voice, not once. For a whole week I can't remember getting angry, not one time. But here I was back at home just as mean as ever.

"Dear God, please help me stop being so angry. I really hate it. Please help me be a nicer person, especially to my sisters. Please help me to know you the way Brett does. I really want to know you, and I really want to be a better person."

I waited a few hours before joining my family again. This time I wasn't yelling or calling anyone names. I found my mom in her sewing room, so I sat down to talk.

"What's up, Honey?" She asked. "You look sad."

"I don't get it mom," I replied. "I don't understand how I can go to camp every year, have a wonderful time, never get angry or raise my voice, then come home and be a horrible person again. I don't understand why this happens to me every year."

I know my mom wanted to help me. I know it hurt her to see me like that. Parents are born with an overwhelming need to make everything okay. My mom was no exception.

She began to tell me that I wasn't as horrible as I thought I was, but she was wrong. She wanted me to feel better, but I was serious. I needed help. I was tired of being frustrated all the time. I wanted to be better, but I didn't know how.

I thought about the message I heard at camp about the Holy Spirit. I remember the speaker saying the Holy Spirit would empower me so I could live victorious.

Why didn't I remember that? I asked myself. *Is that what I was missing?*

My mom knew about the Holy Spirit. I heard her talking about Him before. She didn't mention Him often, but she had to know something.

"Mom," I asked. "What do you know about the Holy Spirit?" I expected a dramatic response, but she barely looked up while she answered.

"We believe the Holy Spirit is the third person of the Trinity, and when we accept Jesus into our hearts, the Holy Spirit comes to dwell within us. He empowers us to live better lives. Jesus gave us His Holy Spirit after he was raised from the dead; after He sat down next to the Father in heaven. God gave Him to us to be our helper, our comforter, and our friend. Why do you ask?"

"Why didn't anyone ever tell me about the Holy Spirit? Here I am, a total mess, and no one has ever shared with me the answer to my problem? Why?"

"I just thought you knew," my mom replied. "You've gone to church your whole life. You should know who the Holy Spirit is."

Well, I didn't. I didn't know a lot of things, and I was extremely discouraged.

My mom suggested I send my aunt Stacey a note. She said she knew a lot about the Bible, and could probably answer all of my questions. She told me my aunt Stacey had an alcohol and cigarette problem, but God delivered her. She thought maybe it was the power of the Holy Spirit that helped her quit.

"Okay," I said. "I'll call aunt Stacey."

I was a little embarrassed calling my aunt to ask her questions about God. I would have to tell her about myself, and I was vain. I didn't really want to tell her all the bad stuff about me.

Most of my friends considered me well behaved, friendly, and all together. My aunt and uncle thought the same. I very seldom let anyone know the real me. Only my mom, dad, and my sisters had the privilege.

When my aunt Stacey answered the phone she sounded really happy to hear from me. I was only home from camp one day and she had already heard from Brett.

"Hi Honey, I'm so glad you called. Brett came by yesterday and told me all about the great time you two had, sounds like he really likes you. He says he's going to call you and ask you out. I'm so excited. He's such a great kid."

"Well, that's sort of why I called," I responded. "Brett is a great guy, but he deserves someone far better than me. He has his life together, and his relationship with God is amazing. I couldn't possibly measure up to the type of girl he needs no matter how hard I try. I'm not the girl for him. I'm just not. I came home from camp wanting to be a better person," I continued. "When I asked my mom what to do, she told me to talk to you. You are my only hope. Please tell me what to do. I so badly want to be a better person."

After a short pause my aunt began, "I was angry, depressed, and an absolute mess," she said. "I went to church every Sunday, youth group every Wednesday, summer and winter camp every year and God knows, every other church activity taking place. I should have known God better than anyone, yet I didn't. I barely knew Him at all."

"Sure, I believed in Him, but I had no idea how to get close to Him. Living victoriously was as foreign to me as it is to you. But look at me now. I have a great relationship with God today. I couldn't get closer to God if I wanted to. I don't think it's possible."

She continued, "God revealed Himself to me in a powerful way and he will do the same for you. I will tell you how. But I'm going to write it in a letter and send it to you. I want you to look it over often. Life gets busy and we need reminders. We need to keep the things of God constantly before our eyes. But first let me ask you a question: Did you know that Jesus is God? Did you know that Jesus was in the beginning with the Father before creation? The first step to a closer relationship with God is to know who He is."

I think I knew that Jesus was God, who didn't? But I didn't understand how He was with the Father in the beginning? Wasn't Jesus born a baby in a manger many years after creation? Wasn't Jesus referred to as God's son? How could God's son be God?

"I don't think I knew that, aunt Stacey. I knew that Jesus was God's son, but how was He with the Father in the beginning? That doesn't make any sense."

"I thought you were going to say that," she responded. "That was my problem too. I knew Jesus as God's son, but I really never understood the concept of the Trinity. I couldn't figure out how Jesus and God was the same person, when they were obviously two different people in the Bible. So I did a study on the three persons of the Trinity, and now it all makes sense. I will send you the same study. Once you understand who God really is, in all three persons, living a victorious life is easier."

When I got off the phone I felt a little better. She really didn't tell me anything helpful right away, but since I knew she was sending me information, I was hopeful. I needed hope. Anything was better than nothing. I was just tired of being who I was.

TURNING AROUND

I had no plans for the day. No one called to make any. I guess it was up to me to let everyone know I was available. By now Cindy was home, so I knew Amelia wouldn't be alone. I really wanted to call my new friends without upsetting her. My cheer friends were so much more fun.

Stephanie was the girl on the team I liked the most. She was simple like me. We attended a few parties together over the summer, and had a lot of fun, so I called her first. She answered and told me to come on over. She said she invited a few friends over to swim and hang out.

"I'll be right there," I said.

I was glad to have somewhere to go. Even though I just returned home the day before, I was not interested in spending time with my mom and sisters. I got really bored at home. I felt cooped up like I was missing out on something.

My mom was always telling me to find something to do, but there was never anything to do—unless, of course, I had my own pool party. But not today; today I was going over to Stephanie's, and I was excited.

I grabbed my suit and towel, called out to my mom, "I'm going over to Stephanie's house to swim," and I ran out the door.

The whole team was at Stephanie's house. I couldn't believe it, everyone was there. I was quite surprised that no one told me about it. I mean, I saw a few girls, Ally and Sarah, at the mall the night before, and neither one of them mentioned the party. I was a little confused. In just one week's time the whole team forgot about me? *What a bunch of arrogant, stuck up people*, I thought. *And these are my friends*?

Needless to say I was frustrated and upset. I felt left out, and I was seriously offended. At first I wanted to run, then I wanted to scream, but finally I decided to hide my feelings. I had to spend the entire year with these girls. Running away was not the answer.

So this is how Amelia and Cindy feel? I thought. *Wow*, I felt horrible.

I only stayed at the party long enough to show my face. I refused to let anyone know how I felt. I was seriously hurt, and resented being there, but there was no way I would let them know.

And I thought I was bad?

That was the longest hour of my life. When it was time to leave, I grabbed my bag and snuck out the door. I didn't say goodbye to anyone. I was so angry I cried all the way home. I couldn't believe they did that to me. As the anger escalated, so did the hatred. Although I knew it wasn't hatred, because that was such a strong word, yet it felt just as rotten.

When I got home I ran straight to my room. The last thing I wanted was to explain to my mom how awful my new friends were. She tried to tell me before and I wouldn't listen. I didn't need her saying she told me so.

I was still curious about Trevor. He called a few times while I was away, but he never left a message. *I'm sure someone told him I was home? Why wasn't he calling? Did he move on?* I asked myself. *No. How could he? We only had one date. There's no way he gave up that quick.*

I wanted to call him. I was afraid if I waited any longer he'd really move on, but I was also afraid of what he might say. When I finally got up the nerve to call him, I got his machine.

"Hi Trevor," I began. "This is Honey. Remember me? I was away all last week. I am so sorry I didn't have a chance to tell you. I actually forgot I was leaving, and when I found out, the morning after our date, I didn't have time to tell anyone. Amelia was supposed to let you know where I was. I hope she did. Anyway, I'm home now, so if you want, you can give me a call. Okay. I guess that's it. Hopefully I will talk to you soon. Goodbye."

Three days passed and I never heard from him. He never called back.

How could he? I asked myself. *How could he just ignore me like that?*

I was heartbroken. I had such a nice time on our first date and was looking forward to spending more time with him during the summer. So you can imagine my disappointment when I discovered he was dating another girl. Her name was Amber. I didn't know her very well, but I heard she was a bit feistier than me.

That's it, I thought. *That's the reason he's with her. He heard I was a good girl, so he chose someone with no morals.* I was so angry.

I wasn't sure what bothered me more: his dating Amber or the fact that no one told me. I had to see them together at the mall. What an unpleasant surprise. I knew something was up when he didn't call, but this? I was clueless. Seeing him with her really hurt, so as soon as I saw them I turned and went the other way. I hoped he didn't see me. I had no desire to talk to him.

What a shame, I thought. *We could have been so good together.*

My friends from the cheer team started calling again. They invited me everywhere: to the beach, swim parties, movies, slumber parties, and hang-a-rounds. At first I said no, I needed time to recover, but after a few weeks I felt better and started saying yes.

I saw Trevor a lot over the summer. He was everywhere I went, and he was always with Amber. A few times he looked at me, but he never said a word. Since I left him a message, the ball was in his court. I had no intentions of speaking first, so we just never spoke. At first it was uncomfortable, but then it got easier. Being on the cheer team meant I had to see him. I had to get over him fast, and I did. Well, sort of I did.

I contemplated calling Brett, but that seemed rude. Just because Trevor and I didn't work out, didn't make it okay to call Brett. In all fairness, I needed to leave him alone.

With cheer practice and all the activities I was invited to, I was never bored, but not having a boyfriend left a hole in my heart. I was much better off before I met Trevor. He was a schmuck who broke my heart; just another reminder to stay far away from boys.

It took Brett three weeks to call me. I often wondered if he would. He seemed interested in getting together, but he wasn't calling, so I concluded he wasn't going to. Because I decided he was better off without me, it was best that he didn't call. So when he did, I was surprised.

He started talking small talk. He didn't say anything important. When he mentioned he was going away on a long summer vacation, and getting together wasn't an option, I was confused. *Then why are you calling*? I thought.

"No problem," I said. "Remember, I told you I was dating someone anyway?"

I lied. Why not? It was easier that way. I let him off the hook, and I felt better. Trevor dumped me and Brett changed his mind—didn't do much for my self esteem. *I'm sure this won't be the last time I have boy trouble*, I thought.

After he shared his plans, I hurried to get off the phone. I was just too devastated to talk anymore.

"Have a great summer," I said sarcastically.

Running up the stairs I burst into tears. I was becoming more disillusioned and discouraged by the minute. Not hearing from Brett was easier than hearing he didn't want to see me. Although he never said that, I knew that's what he meant. Jumping to conclusions didn't help the situation, but all of this rejection was getting to me. I was already feeling badly after what Trevor did. Brett's news only made it worse.

Maybe he was going on a long vacation, I reasoned. *Maybe he told me the truth.* Brett was too good for me anyway and deserved someone better. Isn't that what I thought? So what was my problem? I didn't want him, but I wanted him to want me. How unfair was that? I hated it when my life made no sense.

Stephanie called a few hours later to see if I wanted to go roller-skating. I didn't skate, but it sounded fun.

"Sure," I said. "Let me ask my mom."

Surprisingly, my mom said no. She said it was a dangerous sport and a bad idea.

"What?" I responded. "Dangerous? What are you talking about?"

I got back on the phone and told Stephanie I'd go, "I'll tell my mom we're going to the show."

I didn't feel very good about lying, but my mom was wrong. She was ridiculous and said no for all the wrong reasons. I wasn't a baby anymore and I wasn't in the mood to be treated like one.

Roller-skating was fun. I had only gone one other time when I was younger, but I forgot how much fun it was. We laughed more than I laughed in a long time. I laughed so hard I wet my pants. Roller-skating was definitely what I needed. This was just what the doctor ordered.

I fell down at least a hundred times, over and over again, what a blast. But then something unexpected happened. I fell in an awkward position and twisted my leg. I was flat on my back, and my leg was throbbing in pain.

I started screaming, "Stephanie, my leg is broken. What am I going to do? Quick, call my mom." I didn't know what was worse, the panic or the pain.

My mom is going to kill me.

When the paramedics arrived they picked me up and put me on a stretcher. They said they were taking me to the hospital, but they had to wait for my mom. Since I was a minor, they needed her consent. Once she arrived and gave them permission, they put me in the ambulance and drove me away.

The hospital was close so it wasn't long before I was treated. The doctor gave me a sedative to calm me down and an anesthetic to numb my leg. After the pain went away, he straightened it, and put it in a cast. As he popped my leg back into place I heard the bones crack. It was a horrifying sound.

My mom was actually sympathetic. I wasn't sure if her kindness was real, or if she was just waiting until we got home to let me have it. Either way, I was glad she was there. After the doctor put the cast on my leg, he read me a few instructions and let me go. A nurse helped me out to the car because I couldn't walk alone—the cast was so awkward.

On the way out my mom looked a little disappointed. "Well, Honey, there goes cheerleading."

I never thought about the consequences of a broken leg. How was I going to cheer? How was I going to do anything?

"Next time I tell you no," my mom proceeded, "you might want to listen to me. I usually have good reasons for my decisions. Just because you don't agree with them, doesn't make them wrong. A mother's instinct is usually right so next time, listen to me."

I stayed home a lot in the first few weeks. I couldn't drive. I couldn't swim. I could barely walk around with the crutches. My mom rented me movies and friends came over.

After a few weeks I started venturing out. My friends picked me up and drove me around—just getting out of the house was nice. They willingly helped me. I didn't ask them to, so it felt good to know they cared.

I attended every cheerleading practice. I even went to cheer camp. My mom paid for it in advance, so even though I was disabled, I went anyway. They taught me how to use the megaphone and the microphone. They taught me how to be a yell leader.

"What a great idea." I told the camp instructor.

After camp I mentioned it to my cheer coach and she agreed I was perfect for the job. Maybe I couldn't jump, but everyone knew I could yell.

Cheer practice was always held near the football field. We practiced cheering while the guys played football. I enjoyed watching Trevor. As soon as I quit hating him, watching him was fun again. I often wished we were still dating, but there wasn't anything I could do about it. However, Carl, a friend of Trevor's, began calling me.

A few times while homebound he came by with the girls. I didn't think much of it because he was Trevor's friend, but then he started calling, and we became friends. I didn't see anything wrong with it. Trevor didn't want me, so I was free to date anyone I chose, right?

Carl was outgoing. He stood about 5'8". He weighed a little more then Trevor, but then so did everyone else. Carl's hair and eyes were dark brown. He wasn't as cute as Trevor, but he definitely looked good. I didn't feel the same for him as I did Trevor. We lacked the chemistry, but having a guy friend to hang out with was really nice.

Guy friends were different than girlfriends. I liked it when Carl looked at me like I was pretty. I liked the teasing and the flirting. Girlfriends were great, but they lacked that 'something special' that boys had.

Dating Trevor for only one day ruined me. It gave me a taste of having a boyfriend, and I liked it. Going out with Trevor was exciting: staring at him, thinking about him, knowing he was there. When he dumped me, I was crushed, but Carl filled the void.

Carl started calling two or three times a day just to talk. Before long the hole in my heart disappeared. I still didn't find him physically attractive, but the friendship grew strong. Carl was just as good a friend to me as Stephanie, yet not the same as Amelia and Cindy. No one could ever replace the feelings I had for my two best friends.

My relationship with Carl changed the way I thought about guys. I learned they weren't all creepy idiots. I was determined to keep Carl as a friend though. I refused to let it get serious. There was no way I was ever going to put myself in a vulnerable position again.

The package from aunt Stacey took a long time to arrive. I didn't ask her why because I actually forgot about it. My life got easier and I wasn't as miserable. The information she sent lost its importance, so when it arrived I put it in a drawer. I promised to look at it soon.

Receiving the package got me thinking. *I wonder why I feel better. I wonder if aunt Stacey's been praying for me.*

I felt better after I broke my leg. Friends came over everyday to sit with me. Friends I didn't even know I had were calling and coming by. Then I met Carl. My attitude changed around that time. Having so many friends who actually cared about me, made a huge difference.

Isn't it funny, I thought, *how God can take a bad situation and turn it around for good? Yep. Aunt Stacey's been praying for me.*

When I finally got around to opening the package, that's when I saw the small book titled, "Being Filled." There was also a bunch of papers titled, "Jesus and the Father are one." Looking through the papers I noticed a lot of scriptures with references to Jesus and the Godhead.

I wished I had more time to really read through the material, but feeling better, and having so much to do, I put it back in the drawer. I promised myself again, I would look at it later.

When my aunt Stacey called to see if I received the information, I told her yes. I didn't tell her I was too busy to read it, because she obviously spent a lot of time putting it together. I told her I looked through most of it. I told her the book was next. She was eager to help me, and I didn't want to disappoint her. I mean, I was the one who called her.

"Thank you aunt Stacey," I began. "I appreciate you taking the time to help me. I promise to read the material as soon as possible. You know with cheerleading practices and school starting soon, it might take me awhile, but I will definitely look over it and let you know what I think."

For one brief moment I actually felt like I'd been set free from every care in the world. Nothing was troubling me, not one disturbing thought. *Wow*, I said to myself, *if only I could feel this good forever.*

NEVER AGAIN

One day, shortly after getting my cast off, Carl and I were driving around looking for something to do. We had the radio on loud, and the top to his mom's convertible was down.

We drove around our friend's neighborhoods hoping to find a party, or even just a few people to hang out with. The weather was warmer than usual so we were hoping to find a pool party. We thought about swimming at my house, but wanted to hang out with other people, not just ourselves.

As we drove through Stephanie's tract, I noticed her up in the bonus room window—she had a boy in her arms. Looking closely, I saw it was Trevor.

"What?" I yelled. "Carl, look. It's Stephanie and Trevor. I can't believe it. How long has that been going on? What happened to Amber?"

Carl looked away. He obviously knew something.

"What do you know?" I asked him. "You know something, don't you?"

Carl shook his head, but he was lying. All guys lied. I couldn't believe one of my friends was dating my 'should be' boyfriend, and again, no one told me.

Completely in shock, I asked Carl to take me home. I didn't feel like doing anything anymore, especially with him. He knew about Trevor and Stephanie and didn't tell me.

I ran in the house and called Amelia. "Amelia, you won't believe what I just saw? Stephanie wrapped around Trevor. Can you believe it? How could Stephanie do that to me? She knows how much I like him. She knew how crushed I was when he dumped me. What a terrible person."

The more I thought about it the more confused I was. *Why? What does he see in her?* I understood Amber. I mean, she was cute and easy, from what I heard, but Stephanie? She was no better than me.

Having my heart broken once was bad enough, but twice really hurt, and from the same guy. *I wish I had followed my instincts, and avoided him from the start, stupid me.* I asked Amelia to come over. She said she was on her way.

Amelia was a good friend. It didn't matter how I treated her, she was always there for me. She never said much, and she never rubbed it in. I felt bad spending so much time with Stephanie, ignoring my true friends, and then finding out Stephanie wasn't a real friend at all.

"I'm so sorry I always choose other people over you." I wanted her to know I knew I was rotten.

"I wish I never joined the cheer team. It is an utter nightmare every day. If I wasn't on that team, I would never have met Trevor, or Stephanie, or any of those other awful people. I'm sorry I take our friendship for granted, and I promise to try harder." Amelia just smiled, and I knew she understood.

Carl called to apologize. He said he kept the secret because he didn't want to hurt me. I believed him, but I told him I needed some time. I told him I needed to stay away from him, and all the rest of the gang. I needed to spend a few days just me and my two best friends.

Cindy came over a few hours later and the three of us sat around watching movies and talking. I was glad they were with me. They never made me feel bad about myself. In fact, they always made everything better.

School was starting soon and cheer practices were postponed. Parents complained that their families couldn't go anywhere because of practice. The girls were given two weeks to vacation one last time. I didn't really have anywhere to go, but I desperately needed to get away.

Amelia's cousin was taking a trip to Catalina Island, and she invited ten extra people to help cover the cost. Amelia invited me, and as soon as my parents said yes, my bags were packed and I was ready to go.

Cindy went to another state to visit relatives. She was really upset that she wasn't going with us. I remember one time my family had plans, but my friends were doing something better, so my parents let me go with my friends.

Why were Cindy's parents so strict? She wasn't allowed to try out for cheerleading, she wasn't allowed to go to most parties, and now she had to miss out on the last real adventure before school started. Times like these made me extra grateful for my parents. Of course there were days I hated them, but most of the time they were okay.

I never went very far without my parents, so I was definitely looking forward to the trip. I was a little surprised they said yes. The only one they knew going was Amelia. Everyone else was Amelia's cousin's friends. I guess they trusted her.

Her cousin's name was Sheila. She was a few years older than us. She was about 5'9", blonde hair, and beautiful. I felt extra inadequate walking next to her, but I was so excited about the trip I didn't care. I just wanted to have fun.

The boat ride over to the island was spectacular. That was my favorite part of the whole trip. My mom insisted I take some pills to avoid any chance of sea sickness.

"Honey, I always get seasick. If you're anything like me, you'll get sick too."

But I wasn't like my mom. I never got seasick. I traveled before on a few smaller boats and they never bothered me. This boat, even though large, didn't bother me either. But maybe it's because I took the pills. *Who knows?*

I stood near the front of the boat the entire ride over letting the wind blow through my hair. The mist from the ocean drenched my face, and the sound of the wind was like music. It was glorious. During the ride, nothing mattered. Every care and concern I boarded that boat with vanished.

Thank you mom for allowing me to go on this trip, I yelled out into the air even though I knew she couldn't hear me.

And thank you God for this magnificent time I get to spend away from all the people in my life who make me miserable. I was excited.

Catalina wasn't a big island. I mean, it was big, but the area where we stayed wasn't. Most of the tourist locations were very close to each other. The condo where we stayed was up a hill off the main road. The walk to the beach took about five minutes.

There were four large rooms in the condo with a few beds in each. There was also a couch bed in the living room where Sheila volunteered to sleep. Amelia and I grabbed one of the rooms near the front of the condo. Out the window was a perfect view of the ocean.

Because my leg was in a cast for four weeks my body was still weak and tired. I didn't get much exercise sitting around all that time, so I planned to walk a lot and eat well. I had the whole week planned out: I would lie out in the sun from morning until night, and eat fruit. Early in the morning, and before the sun went down, I would walk.

That was the plan and Amelia agreed. She too wanted a nice relaxing time away from home. She liked the idea of lying out in the sun and eating healthy. So it was settled:

sun, walks and fruit. Sheila made different plans. Her thoughts were solely on the nightlife. During the day, she too spent time in the sun, but when evening came, she was ready to party.

None of us were old enough to get into the nightclubs. Even Sheila's friends were too young. She wasn't happy about clubbing by herself, so we all went, but instead of going in, we all sat outside, so she was not alone. It was obvious Sheila was looking for a man.

Night after night we sat outside the clubs checking out guys. Every night Sheila went off with someone new, and then Amelia and I would go back to our room. Our last night Sheila met two guys both eager to hang out with her. I knew she was going to ask me to hang out too, and although I had no intentions of saying yes, it was hard to say no. Sheila was extremely manipulating, and I was easily intimated.

I don't know why I cared so much about what people thought of me. I was afraid Sheila would be mad if I said no, so I allowed her to put me in a very uncomfortable situation.

That was one thing I hated about myself, yet I couldn't seem to change. I remember on many occasions trying to say no and feeling tremendous amounts of guilt. Saying no was uncomfortable, so I just said yes.

Thank God Amelia knew me well. I just knew she had my back, but instead, she gave me a big hug, and went back to the condo.

"I'm tired Honey," she said. "I'll see you later."

I couldn't believe she left me there with her cousin and two strange men. I watched her walk away with my mouth wide open, in shock. I turned around in my chair and just stared at Sheila. Couldn't she see the dread in my eyes?

Up until that night, I was drinking cherry coke, but during the confusion of the situation, Sheila ordered me a rum and coke. When I took a drink of what I thought was my soda, I cringed.

I wasn't a drinker, nor did I want to become one, so I was not expecting rum in my glass, but once again it was easier to drink it than to tell her no. One drink turned into three, and within an hour I was drunk.

The two men sitting with us were at least ten years older. They were nice looking men, but entirely too old. Well, maybe not for Sheila, who appeared to like older men, but definitely for me. I was not having a good time, but as the alcohol built up in my system, the thought of hanging out with thirty-year-olds, wasn't so bad.

After a few hours of talking, the two men invited Sheila and I to their boat. They had a large sized vessel docked in the harbor, but it wasn't near the landing board. We had to take a jet ski.

I was frightened in a way I had never felt before. Here I was on a boat, in the middle of the ocean, that I knew I could not get off of, with two strange men who were drunk.

"Oh my God," I shouted. "I don't feel so well."

I leaned over the side of the boat and began to heave. I started throwing up and I couldn't stop. It was not a pretty site. After I was finished one of the men put me on the Jet Ski and took me back to land.

I started running as fast as I could to the condo. When I got there I ran in the room and started screaming at Amelia, "I can't believe you left me there. You just left me there with your cousin and two strange men. What is wrong with you? I could've been killed." I was so glad we were going home the next day. If there was a way to get home that night I would have taken it.

Of course Amelia was deeply sorry. I don't think she quite understood the type of person her cousin was, or maybe she had more confidence in me. Anyway, she must have apologized a hundred times, so I forgave her. I didn't want to, because I felt so betrayed, but I did anyway.

The next morning I had what I supposed was a hangover—my head hurt and my stomach was sick. I swore to never drink again and I meant it. Not only did the alcohol taste bad, it made me feel bad too. *Why in the world does anyone want to drink?* It was nasty, so nasty, that every time I thought about it, it made me sick again.

The boat ride home wasn't as delightful as the ride there. I was not feeling well at all. I didn't get seasick on the way home, because I was already sick. But honestly, who could tell the difference. I missed standing outside letting the wind rush through my hair. I just sat in a chair the whole way home pouting because I was so weak.

I wish I could learn to say no, I thought. *I wish I could learn to stand up for myself and quit letting everyone walk all over me.*

After we left the boat we drove the hour home in silence. Amelia's cousin never said one word to me; she didn't even ask me how I was. *How selfish,* I said to myself. *Maybe I should pray for her?* It was good to be home again. I always felt the same after every trip. I was happy to leave, but even happier to be home.

This trip left a bad feeling I could not shake. I was shocked that I allowed myself to drink until I got drunk, and it scared me that I almost got stranded with a guy I'd never met. Over again in my mind I played out the scenario. *Do you know Honey what could have happened to you if you had not gotten sick?* The more I thought about it, the worse I felt.

I wasn't the nicest person in the world and I knew it. I loved God, but I wasn't the kindest or the most patient. I had plenty of faults. But I knew I wanted to remain pure until my wedding day. It wasn't like I thought I was some spiritual dynamo who would receive special gifts from God for being good. It was just very important to me.

My mom instilled in me at a young age that sleeping with a man before marriage could spoil the marriage to the man I would spend the rest of my life with. The thought of almost losing my purity to some stranger hurt my soul. It was a nightmare I never wanted to experience again.

It was close to dinner when I finally unpacked my things, cleaned up, and got ready for bed. I had no intentions of going out that night. It was Sunday, and school was starting on Wednesday.

I wasn't sure why they always started school in the middle of the week. It had something to do with Memorial Day, or was it Labor Day? Well, one of those holidays was happening the next day and school was starting in three days.

I was excited, yet afraid as always. New situations made me nervous, and although I already knew everyone, I would still have to get used to new classrooms and new teachers. Change was not easy for me.

Hanging around the house for a few days gave me plenty of time to think. It also gave me time to look over the information aunt Stacey sent. I yelled downstairs to my mom, "I'm going to be in my room for awhile. I'll come down for dinner later." I wasn't very hungry. I was still suffering from the hangover. *My God, will this thing ever go away?*

While I looked through the papers I thought about life and how unpredictable it was. Who would have thought a nice peaceful week on an island with my friend could turn out to be such a disaster?

Since Sheila made it back to the condo in one piece, those men probably weren't rapists or serial killers, but that's not to say the next time she'd be so lucky. She took off with a new guy every night. How was she to know she'd come back alive? That night really got me thinking.

MAKING IT RIGHT

Aunt Stacey said the first step to becoming more like God was to know Him. She mentioned that Jesus was with God in the beginning. She had a list of Bible references all proving that the Son of God was actually God in the flesh, and even lived with the Father before creation.

One scripture she listed was John 17:5. It read, "And now, Father (Jesus speaking) glorify me in your presence with the glory I had with you before the world began." *What a great verse*, I thought. *I should spend more time reading the Bible. I bet there is a lot in there I don't know.*

The more I read, the more intrigued I was. Scripture after scripture talked about Jesus and the Father as one. After reading through those which spoke of the Deity of Christ, I read about the Holy Spirit.

Jesus told his disciples he would send them a helper when he ascended into heaven. He sent them a comforter to dwell with them; the promised Holy Spirit. The

Holy Spirit was just as much God as the Father and Jesus. They were three distinct persons in one God-head. I liked that. I spent the rest of the evening reading about the power given to us by God's Spirit.

I needed more help to stay out of trouble, and to keep me out of danger. After the week in Catalina I was convinced I needed more of God to get through life. Although I was mostly concerned with getting through the twelfth grade, I could already foresee that life was going to be a huge challenge, and I needed all the help I could get.

Every year, right before school started, my mom took my sisters and I shopping for new clothes. This year she split the nights up so that only one of us went with her at a time. I definitely liked it better that way. My mom and I went to the mall and spent three hours looking through all of my favorite stores. After buying clothes and shoes we stopped off at the ice cream parlor and had a hot fudge sundae--my favorite.

I hadn't spent much time with my mom during the summer. I know she wanted me home more, but I also knew she understood. I think my mom remembered her teenage years, because she was very patient with my sisters and I. It was good spending time with her shopping and eating ice cream.

We talked a lot about Trevor and Brett. I shared with her what happened between me and Stephanie. I told her many things about the summer, but I did not share with her what happened in Catalina. I decided that situation was best left unsaid. As it was, my mom didn't worry much about me. Sharing that story would change everything, and since I vowed to be more careful, there wasn't any reason to concern her.

When we returned home, I tried on all my new clothes. I needed to make sure I still liked them. I was fickle that way. I would put aside any outfit I was unsure of and try in on for Amelia. Sometimes I just needed a second opinion. This was my last year of school. I was going to be a senior and a cheerleader. I needed to look my best. Luckily, every piece of clothing looked just as good as it did when I bought it, so I hung each outfit in my closet confident I was ready to start school.

The day before school started was the worst. Anxiety set in and I spent the whole day in the bathroom. My mom told me to think of something else.

"Honey," she began, "if you change your thinking you'll feel better. Try reminiscing about the beach or summer camp."

I know she meant well, but she wasn't helping. How in the world was I to think of the beach when school was starting the next day. What was she thinking? I was just praying that my stomach would calm down before the morning. "Please God; don't let me go to school tomorrow with the runs."

Every year was the same. No matter how hard I tried to prepare for the first day, I was always a nervous wreck. If I wasn't on the cheer team I'm certain I'd beg once again to be home-schooled. Every year I asked, and every year my mom said no. One last time

I opened my closet to glance over my new outfits. *What should I wear tomorrow?* I thought. *I guess I'll decide in the morning.*

I was a little nervous about seeing Stephanie. I hadn't seen her since that terrible day when she was wrapped around Trevor. We only had one cheer practice before the end of summer, and she didn't show up. I was certain she was afraid to face me. *How could she not be?* I thought. *I know I would be, but then I would never do that to one of my friends.*

In my opinion what she did was horrible. I wasn't sure I wanted to forgive her, although I knew I would, because I always did. Holding grudges just wasn't my thing. As for Trevor, I felt I was over him. He lost out. I imagined us spending the entire year together; becoming each others best friend; hanging out at lunch and going for hamburgers after the games. But he blew it. Now he was stuck with Stephanie, and I was glad.

I knew she'd never be the girlfriend for Trevor that I was. I sensed our chemistry on the very first date. We got along really well right from the start, and that was a good sign. It's just too bad he didn't see it that way. I was ready to move on. I was certain to meet plenty of other eligible guys now that I was a cheerleader and part of the in-crowd. I just wished I felt better; a little less hopeless.

Right before bed Amelia called to see how I was. She knew I suffered terribly from stomach problems, and wanted to give me her condolences.

"Thanks, Amelia," I said. "It's always good to know my friends feel my pain. It's too bad you can't suffer for me, just kidding."

No matter what happened, Amelia was always there for me. Even after the argument we had in Catalina, we were still as close as ever. And then I thought about Aubrey. *That's strange*, I thought. *I wonder how Aubrey is.*

Aubrey and I never saw each other outside of church or camp. We just never hung out. It was strange that I was thinking about her. I never thought about her. *Maybe I'll give her a call tomorrow and see how she is. I bet she'd like that.*

By the time I crawled into bed, my stomach was feeling a little better. *Maybe if I don't eat anything in the morning, I'll be okay.* Within a few minutes of lying down, right before I slowly drifted off to sleep, my phone rang. It was aunt Stacey.

"Hi Honey, how are you?"

"I'm good," I responded, "just now going to bed. Tomorrow's the big first day of school. Midnight rendezvous are now over for the next nine months. What's up?" Aunt Stacey never called just to call. I knew she had a reason.

"I was just calling to let you know Brett's been asking about you. He came back from his trip just a few days ago, and I saw him this past Sunday at church. The first thing he asked me was how you were. I said I didn't know because I hadn't talked to you in a while, but I told him I'd give you a call and find out. So, how are you?"

"I'm fine," I replied. "I really don't know what to say."

I felt awkward. I knew my aunt adored Brett, but I wasn't feeling the same way. I mean, yeah, he was a great guy, but just not for me.

"Tell him I'm doing well and maybe I'll get a chance to come visit someday. Although with school and cheerleading it'll be hard. Tell him hi for me, okay?"

I could tell she sensed my disinterest because she quickly changed the subject. We talked a few minutes about school and summer, and I thanked her again for sending the information. I told her I had a chance to look it over, but not to really study it. She told me to let her know if I needed any other info, and then we got off the phone. I was sound to sleep within only a few short minutes.

The morning came far too quickly. Waking up everyday all summer at noon made it difficult to get up at seven thirty.

"No!" I hollered. "I can't wake up this early. It's too early. Leave me alone. I don't want to get up."

Mornings were not my favorite time of day, especially this early. After my dad came in a few more times—with no luck—he grabbed my blankets and pulled them off of me.

"Now, get up!" he yelled. "It's time to get up. You have to drop your sister off first, so get up. You don't have anymore time to lie there."

It felt good to be back at school once I got settled in. My first thought was always, *how did I look and who looked better than me?* I was told that the cheerleaders were to wear their uniforms the first day of school, but I didn't. I had a whole closet full of brand new clothes, there was no way I was wearing my uniform. I was in hopes some of the other girls had banned the idea as well, but I was the only one.

I decided to clear the air with Stephanie. I didn't want any feelings of un-forgiveness harbored in my heart, not even for a day. It was easy during the summer because I didn't have to see her, but now I'd see her all the time. The tension between us was very uncomfortable, so I decided to forgive her and let it go.

I also decided that if the moment presented itself I would talk to Trevor. All summer I avoided him, but again, here at school, it would be very difficult. Ironically, Stephanie and Trevor were both in my homeroom class, and they were not sitting next to each other.

I approached Stephanie as soon as I walked into the room. "I'm sorry Stephanie that I was mad at you for dating Trevor." She just stared at me. "I realize I have no control over who Trevor likes, and if it's you, then I shouldn't blame you."

When I finished my apology Stephanie smiled and said, "thank you, Honey." I could tell by the look on her face she was more relieved than I was. Trevor was a different story. As soon as I saw him I was mad all over again. *He might be a little harder*, I said to myself. *I can't believe he dumped me like that, and hasn't said one word about it. He's had all summer to explain and he acts like nothing happened.* I was furious.

I decided to wait until I calmed down before talking to Trevor. My emotions would definitely get in the way and he'd see how angry I was. I obviously still liked him, but I really wished I didn't.

The day went great. I saw all my old friends. Of course I saw most of them over the summer, but there were plenty of others I hadn't seen since the last day of my junior year. I had a lot of friends, or should I say, a lot of people knew me.

I never thought of myself as popular, but as I walked around campus everybody was shouting, "Hi Honey." I couldn't walk two feet without hearing someone shout my name. As hard as I tried to be invisible—it just wasn't working.

I enjoyed my classes. Since I already had most of the units I needed to graduate, I took fun classes like photography and cooking. My mom told me to take college prep courses. She said it would help me get into college, but I refused. Twelve years of school was a lot and I was tired of learning. I did take a few harder classes like chemistry and Spanish, but I didn't need six advanced placement courses. Didn't she know my head would explode?

I hoped Amelia and Cindy were in some of my classes, but surprisingly they weren't. Amelia was in Spanish, which was good. She spoke the language fluently and helped me a lot, but other than that, neither was in any of the others. Stephanie was in two, and Carl was in three. Trevor was only in my homeroom. I was glad about that.

Lunchtime was great. Although a lot of students left campus, most of my friends hung around the grass area outside the cafeteria. We all bought hamburgers or pizza from the deli window and ate together under a tree. I couldn't believe I was so apprehensive about starting school. That first day could not have been any better. I prayed the remaining days would be just as good.

After school I had cheer practice. I was used to hanging around the parking lot, chatting with friends, and going home when I wanted. Now I had to be there most of the afternoon. I wasn't one who liked commitments, but I promised myself I wouldn't complain until I had something to complain about. As it was, I had nothing else going on. Stephanie, who was a cheerleader the two years prior, said she loved it. I prayed I'd grow to love it too.

MAKES NO SENSE

As soon as I walked into the girl's locker room my friend Meghan, who I knew from church, ran over and asked if I'd heard about Aubrey?

"No," I replied. "I didn't hear anything. I was just thinking about her last night though, which I thought was strange, but no one said anything. Why? What's wrong?"

Now I was really freaked out. What if God was trying to tell me something? What if God put Aubrey on my mind for a reason? The pastor at my church mentioned that sometimes God gives us a thought because He wants us to pray about something—God puts the burden on us to pray.

What if I was supposed to pray and I didn't? I hoped Aubrey was okay.

"Aubrey and her little sister were in a car accident," Meghan began. "Aubrey is in the hospital, but her little sister was killed. They said she died instantly from a head wound. Aubrey wasn't wearing her seatbelt and was thrown from the car. She suffered quite a few broken bones and her head is completely bandaged."

"How terrible," I shouted. "What should I do?"

I quickly ran into the coach's office, "Miss Herbert, a friend of mine was in a bad car accident. Is it okay if I miss practice so I can go see her? Her little sister was killed."

"Of course you can go," she answered.

Although Aubrey and I barely saw each other, she was still a special friend of mine. There was no way I wasn't going to see her. As soon as I got into my car I called my mom, "Mom, guess what? Aubrey was in a bad car accident and she's in the hospital. Her sister was killed and I guess her body is badly broken up."

I started crying before I finished the sentence. I couldn't believe she lost her little sister. I couldn't imagine what that was like. I didn't always appreciate my sisters, but I sure didn't want them to die. Before I got off the phone, my mom told me to drive safe.

When I got to the hospital, Aubrey's mom and a few other ladies were standing outside. You could tell she was crying; her face was red and swollen. The other ladies were crying as well, which made me cry.

"Hi Mrs. White, I'm so sorry about your children. I have no idea what to say. All I can think of is how horrible and tragic. I came to see Aubrey. Is it okay to go in?"

Aubrey's mother excused herself from her friends and walked me into the hospital. She put her arm around my shoulders and began softly explaining what had happened. She warned me that Aubrey had a bandage wrapped around her head and not to be alarmed. At first I was concerned, now I was scared. I wished my mom was with me, but she had to pick up my sisters from school. Aubrey was lying in a bed near the window. She was the only patient in there.

"Wow Aubrey," I said. "You get a private room—how lucky." I didn't really know what to say. I just felt so bad for her. Her mom was right. Her whole head was bandaged and all I could see was her eyes, her nose and a slit where her mouth was.

I sat down in a chair next to her and decided to stay awhile—I needed to be there. Aubrey was a good friend. Every year at camp she'd stay close to me so I never felt alone. I wanted her to feel just as safe. She understood me, and for that reason, I wanted to be there for her.

"Thanks Honey for coming."

That was all I needed to hear.

Time went by slowly there in the hospital. Aubrey slept most of the day and had only two other visitors. Nearly all of her family and friends were preparing for her little sister's memorial service.

Funerals were very difficult for me. I went to only one other, and it was very sad; a lot sadder than I expected. The deceased was an older lady, a friend of my moms. I didn't even know her, but watching her friends and family suffer from their loss, was unbearable. I knew the funeral for an eleven-year-old girl would be far worse. There was no way I was going. As long as Aubrey was in the hospital, my place was with her.

That night as I lay in bed, I thought about my day and how weird it was. It all started out so well. I enjoyed school very much. I was excited about my classes. I even made amends with Stephanie. Then the news about Aubrey came and everything changed.

I woke up early the next morning to get my homework done and wondered how I would make it all work. After school there was cheer, then the hospital. My plan was to get home in time to do homework before bed. I wondered when I'd have time for anything else.

Shame on you Honey, I thought. *You need to count your blessings.*

The next day was hard. I couldn't stop thinking about Aubrey. It was awful that someone as nice as her had to suffer such a horrible tragedy. I wondered why God allowed accidents to happen. My pastor explained that God didn't make bad things happen, but they happened because we live in a fallen world.

Aubrey didn't go to my school, she was home-schooled. So the school didn't honor her. Most of the students didn't even know who she was, so I walked the campus that day feeling lost and alone. No one else shared my pain, and that was okay. I understood. There were a few people like Meghan, and her friends, who knew Aubrey from church, as I did, but not many.

I wished school was over so I could leave. My stomach hurt and I wanted to go home. But of course I had cheer practice and I was certain the coach would make me stay. I didn't ask to leave, however, the coach did ask about Aubrey, which I thought was nice.

"She'll be in the hospital for awhile," I said. "But because her injuries are mainly surface, and not internal, a quick recovery was expected."

Practice was actually good for me. It helped get my mind off of Aubrey. We practiced our dance routines to loud music which I found to be quite comforting. I loved loud music. Whenever I was having a bad day, or life wasn't going my way, I turned the music up really loud. It took my mind off of the circumstances.

After practice I sat in my car for about ten minutes, closed my eyes, and drifted away. I pictured myself with Trevor in a boat on the lake up in the mountains. It was such a peaceful place. I wished I was there. I wished I was anywhere but where I was.

For a few weeks I tried to visit Aubrey everyday. Some days I stayed late. Most days I was the only one there. Occasionally her mom stayed late, but she was suffering immensely from the loss of her daughter—and rightfully so. On the days when she visited Aubrey in the afternoon—while I was there—I felt very uncomfortable. I never knew what to say, so we just sat in silence.

I quietly prayed, "God forbid that a mother should ever have to suffer from the loss of her child again."

Was there anything worse?

My mom suggested I spend less time at the hospital. "I don't want your grades to suffer so close to the beginning of school," she said. "Once you fall behind it'll be very hard to catch up."

She was right. My schoolwork was already piling up. Although most of my classes were easy, they still required extra work. I planned to do it in the hospital while visiting, but when I was there, we watched TV. There was no way I could study chemistry with the television on.

After Aubrey's second week in the hospital I informed her I could only visit a few days a week, instead of everyday. She understood.

During the first month of school the Red Cross came to our campus so students could donate blood. My mom said it was a good idea. "What if Aubrey needed blood after her accident and there wasn't any? That's why people give blood—you should to. You'll feel good about yourself if you do. I promise."

When I went into the room to give blood the lady asked if I'd eaten anything. I hadn't, but I said yes. She told me if I hadn't eaten I couldn't give blood—so I lied. I wasn't watching my weight or anything, I just didn't eat breakfast. I hated eating in the morning.

When it was my turn I sat in a chair and the nurse put a long needle in my arm. She taped it down and left it there for awhile. It felt like forever. When she was done she told me to sit a few minutes and have a glass of orange juice. I told her I felt fine. I didn't want any juice so I left, but I only got as far as the cafeteria stairs before I passed out. When I woke up I was sprawled out on the cement.

I was embarrassed. I was wearing a skirt and high heels—thankfully my skirt wasn't up over my head, however, my shoes were off my feet. It reminded me of a romance novel where the girl passes out from exhaustion, and is rescued by a handsome man, carried onto a bed, and awakens to find a gorgeous hunk standing over her.

However, when I woke up there wasn't any gorgeous anything standing over me, just the janitor and a few of the band members who were practicing nearby. I couldn't believe my mom talked me into giving blood. She was so in trouble.

As the news of my fainting traveled around the school, everyone was laughing. My friends turned it into a joke and made fun of me. *What a bunch of immature little children we have around here,* I thought. Amelia and Cindy were the only two who didn't turn my shame into public humiliation. I was grateful for them. But then at the end of the day Trevor met me in the parking lot and told me he was sorry I fell. I was more than a little shocked.

"Thank you Trevor," I said, "Thank you for taking the time to tell me that."

For a moment I was pleased, but then I thought, *I can't believe you are telling me you feel sorry for me because I passed out, yet you haven't said one word about dumping me for Amber and Stephanie?* Could it be that guys are just stupid? Could it be that they are oblivious to what they do? I didn't understand them and finally accepted I never would.

"So Trevor, how have you been?"

I didn't really care how he was. I was more interested in what he was thinking. I wanted to talk about what happened, but I knew it was best to wait. I didn't want to scare him off before we had a chance to really talk again.

I understood that guys weren't into talking about feelings and the past. They just wanted to forget and go forward. But I wasn't made that way. I wanted to know what happened. If I didn't still care for him I would've let it go. But I thought about him all the time. *Why couldn't I just be interested in Carl?* I thought. *Life would be so much easier.*

Carl and I had a great relationship. He cared for me. But I wasn't physically attracted to him. I know that was hard for him because he really liked me, but I couldn't get past my feelings for Trevor.

It didn't seem to bother Trevor that Carl and I were friends—I think he would have said something by now. I'm certain he knew Carl and I spent time together—they were good friends, but he never mentioned it. Anyway, it was Trevor I wanted to date, and I sure wished he felt the same way.

As I stood there in the parking lot with him, my mind raced with things I wanted to say, but the only words that came out of my mouth were, "I have to go to the hospital and visit my friend Aubrey." *Why do you sabotage everything?* I thought.

Trevor stood silent for a few seconds then said, "Okay Honey. Maybe we can talk tomorrow."

"Sure," I said. "That sounds great."

I got into my car and drove off with a smile as big as the ocean. Trevor wanted to talk. I was thrilled.

That day when I got to the hospital a few of Aubrey's neighbors were visiting. I stayed only for a little while as I felt like an intruder. I gave her a kiss on the hand and told her I'd return in a few days. She seemed a little happier. I was glad.

I wanted so bad to snap my fingers and make time go backwards to the day before the accident. I hated seeing her lying there for so long and there wasn't anything I could do to fix it. I just kept praying and asking God to heal her quickly.

A NEW BEGINNING

I wasn't sure if it was the situation with Trevor or Aubrey's accident that sent me spiraling downward, but I found myself in a bad state of despair. I didn't understand completely what I felt, but I knew something was wrong. All of a sudden I had no desire to do anything, and I felt sad and very tired.

My mom said it sounded like I was depressed. She said it was to be expected after a traumatic experience. "But what was so troubling about my life?" I asked her. "Mine is good. I'm the lucky one."

She said because I was an overly sensitive person I carried the burden of Aubrey and her family. She said it was normal to feel this way for someone I cared about. All I knew was I had no desire to live and I definitely didn't want to be a cheerleader anymore.

I knew not to bring that up to my mom. I was certain to get the commitment lecture I usually got when I wanted to quit something. I was hoping that this time she'd understand because of the circumstances. I mean, it was her who said I suffered because of Aubrey's misfortune. She's the one who said I was probably depressed.

I waited until after dinner that night before I approached her, and I made sure my eyes were red and swollen from crying—I had to set the perfect stage. Lately I hated cheerleading, and I wanted out. I needed my mom's support. She had to know I was serious. When I asked for her permission, she softly replied, "Yes. That is probably a good idea."

I couldn't believe it. She said yes. No lecture. No 'here we go again' speech. All she said was yes. I gave her a hug and said, "Thank you, mom."

That night as I was lying in bed, I thought about Aubrey and how important she was to me. I thought about how great it was to know her. I wanted to spend more time with her after she got out of the hospital. The time spent with her lately definitely strengthened our friendship and we were growing closer everyday.

I couldn't wait to tell Amelia and Cindy I was quitting the cheer team. I knew they'd be more excited than I was. They hated the girls on the team and rightfully so—I wasn't very fond of them anymore myself. As soon as school ended that day I went straight to miss Herbert to tell her I quit— I didn't waste one second. It felt like a forty ton weight lifted off of my shoulders. I felt better than I had in months.

Miss Herbert was a nice lady, maybe forty years old. She didn't have a problem with me quitting, but she sure made me feel guilty. She talked about how much she'd miss me and heavily stressed how the team would never be the same without me. I'm sure I was the nicest one, and I understood her feelings, but no amount of manipulation was going to make me change my mind. And, I was so convinced I made the right decision, I had no concern at all that I'd regret it later—it wasn't possible.

Suddenly my outlook on life changed. I felt I had options. Cheerleading was time consuming and took up most of my summer. I didn't want to lose my whole senior year to it too. Even though I had a lot of fun with the girls, it was still too much. Because of cheerleading I neglected my family, I practically alienated my two best friends, and worst of all, I put God second to everything. My life was about to get better—I could feel it.

But I was even more excited to talk to Trevor. He said he wanted to talk. I waited all summer for this moment and anticipated the best—not the worst—for a change. Yet he wasn't at school that day. I wanted to call him, but I knew that would be entirely too intrusive. If the conversation in anyway went towards us, I was going to tell him how I felt. I wanted him to know I liked him. I didn't want anymore games. If he wanted to get back together with me I was willing.

Amelia told me I was stupid. She said if he broke my heart twice, he could do it again. I tried to explain how it wasn't his fault. "Remember, Amelia, I went away for a week and never answered my phone. How would I feel if he did that to me? I'm sure he got the impression I wasn't interested. You were going to tell him that I was away, but you said you never saw him. God only knows what he was thinking. No wonder he started dating Amber. He had no idea what was going on. Can you blame him?"

For a while after Trevor dumped me I was hurt, but I understood the circumstances. I wasn't upset with him so much because of that, but because after I got home, and left him a message, he never called me back. That's what really bothered me. All I wanted was a chance to explain. I wanted us to talk about what happened.

Maybe it was a guy thing. I heard that guys don't like conflict. They'll avoid it at any cost. Maybe that's what happened—he felt bad and didn't know what to say. I didn't like it, but at least that made sense.

Trevor was away from school for the whole week. Carl said he was sick. I wished we were still friends. I would've taken him something special and sat with him in the afternoons, but I couldn't. We weren't friends yet. Carl told me Trevor mentioned wanting to talk to me. I could tell by the look in his eyes that was hard for him to say.

"Don't worry Carl," I told him. "I'll still love you." I gave him a hug and a kiss on the cheek. "Why God," I asked, "couldn't I be more attracted to Carl? He is such a great guy."

Aubrey spent a total of nine weeks in the hospital. She mentioned there was a strong possibility that she would walk with a cane for awhile. She had a limp from the broken bones and even with all the physical therapy she still had trouble.

My mom used to tell me all the time that life was unpredictable, but who really listens to that kind of talk. I wasn't old enough to deal with such devastating realities, although I guess God thought I was. There I stood in the midst of a reality I found very hard to understand.

Maybe my world thus far had been isolated enough that bad car accidents only happened on television. I know up until that time, except for an occasional selfish outburst of emotional trauma, my life ran rather smoothly. People I knew were okay. I mean, my grandpas had died, but that was expected. Old people were supposed to die.

My aunt Stacy had suffered from a bad alcohol problem—my mom talked about it all the time. I didn't give it much thought though. I didn't see her often enough to care, especially since there wasn't anything I could do. And she was better now. She didn't drink anymore.

I guess I thought in my world everyone got better over time. But Aubrey's little sister wasn't ever coming home and she would never be the same. That was a truth I wasn't ready for and one I wished would go away.

I thought after a few months I'd feel better, but nine weeks later I still felt bad. Instead of spending quality time with Aubrey chatting about boys or playing board games, I sat in a chair and watched television. I wasn't very good company. I was depressed and felt terrible.

I wished I were back at camp; just Aubrey and I sitting on the bank near the lake staring at the water and enjoying the quiet.

"Why God did my friend get into an accident?" I prayed. "Why did it have to be her?"

I cried all the way home from her house that night, and went to bed without any dinner. I was exhausted. I had too many unresolved issues and I couldn't make sense of any of them, so I went to bed. That seemed like the perfect answer for the evening, and it was.

Now that Aubrey was home I was certain she'd be back at church soon. I knew she had lots of friends who cared for her and she'd be back to her old way of living and doing things. I was happy for her. I promised myself everyday I'd stay in touch. I wanted our friendship to grow, not go back to the way it was. Now that cheerleading was over I'd have more time. I was so glad I quit.

Amelia and Cindy were very supportive of me during the few months Aubrey was in the hospital. They didn't know her well, but they did know of her. I appreciated my friends. I hoped they knew that.

I was very anxious to talk to Trevor when he finally returned, "Whatever could have ailed you for that long?" I asked him. "I hope you're okay?"

He smiled and told me he felt better. He said he was going to call, but his throat hurt too bad to talk. I believed him.

I told him I could wait until he was better, but he assured me he felt fine and after school was the best time—before football practice. I said great and went on to class. I knew it was going to be a wonderful day.

I never wanted to be the type of girl who based all her happiness on what was happening with the guy in her life. Life was disappointing, and then Trevor wanted to talk, so life wasn't disappointing anymore? I hated that. I wanted to be happy no matter what Trevor was doing, but I wasn't. Unfortunately, maybe I was one of those girls who loved too much.

It didn't take long before we were an item. He apologized for all that he did and assured me it would never happen again. I had no reason not to believe him. Trevor was a good guy. He had a lot of friends. He had qualities about him I found endearing, however, he did not portray a love for God like Brett did, and no matter how much I enjoyed his company, something was always missing.

www.ingramcontent.com/pod-product-compliance
Lightning Source LLC
Chambersburg PA
CBHW071208130626
46555CB00004B/1624